FORT WORTH LIBRARY

3 1668 05059 0006

W9-AAW-289

LARGE PRINT FICTION KLEYPAS
   2010
Kleypas, Lisa
Christmas Eve at Friday
   Harbor
Southwest   01/06/2011

SOUTHWEST REGIONAL

Christmas Eve
·······································
AT FRIDAY HARBOR

**Center Point
Large Print**

Also by Lisa Kleypas
and available from Center Point Large Print:

Seduce Me at Sunrise
Tempt Me at Twilight

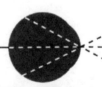

**This Large Print Book carries the
Seal of Approval of N.A.V.H.**

Christmas Eve
AT FRIDAY HARBOR

LISA KLEYPAS

CENTER POINT PUBLISHING
THORNDIKE, MAINE

This Center Point Large Print edition
is published in the year 2010 by arrangement with
St. Martin's Press.

Copyright © 2010 by Lisa Kleypas.

All rights reserved.

This is a work of fiction. All of the characters,
organizations, and events portrayed in
this novel are either products of the author's
imagination or are used fictitiously.

The text of this Large Print edition is unabridged.
In other aspects, this book may vary
from the original edition.
Printed in the United States of America
on permanent paper.
Set in 16-point Times New Roman type.

ISBN: 978-1-60285-939-5

Library of Congress Cataloging-in-Publication Data

Kleypas, Lisa.
Christmas Eve at Friday Harbor / Lisa Kleypas. — Center Point large print ed.
p. cm. — (Friday Harbor series)
Originally published: New York : St Martins Press, 2010.
ISBN 978-1-60285-939-5 (library binding : alk. paper)
1. Family secrets—Fiction. 2. Brothers and sisters—Fiction.
3. San Juan Island (Wash.)—Fiction. 4. Domestic fiction. 5. Christmas stories.
6. Large type books. I. Title. II. Series.
PS3561.L456C47 2010
813'.54—dc22

2010035028

To Ireta and Harrell Ellis

For showing me what love is,
and for living it every day.

Love always,
L.K.

Prologue

Dear Santa

I want just one thing this year
A mom
Plese dont forget I live in friday
harbor now.
thank you

love
Holly

One

• •

Until his sister's death, Mark Nolan had treated his niece Holly with the usual offhand affection of a bachelor uncle. He had seen her during the occasional holiday gatherings, and he'd always made certain to buy her something for her birthday and for Christmas. Usually gift cards. That had been the limit of his interactions with Holly, and it had been enough.

But everything changed one rain-slicked April night in Seattle, when Victoria had been killed in a car wreck on I-5. Since Victoria had never mentioned a will or any plans she had made for Holly's future, Mark had no idea what would happen to her six-year-old daughter. There was no father in the picture. Victoria had never divulged who he was, even to her close friends. Mark was fairly certain that she had never told the father about Holly's existence.

When Victoria had first moved to Seattle, she had fallen in with a bohemian crowd, a group of musicians and creative types. This had resulted in a string of short-term relationships that had provided all the artistic razzle-dazzle Victoria had craved. Eventually, however, she had been forced to admit that the quest for personal fulfillment had to be balanced with a regular paycheck. She'd applied for a job at a software company and had gotten one in human resources, with decent pay and great benefits. Unfortunately by that time, Victoria had found out she was pregnant.

"It's better for everyone if he's not involved," she had told Mark when he had asked who the guy was.

"You need some help with this," Mark had protested. "At the very least, the guy should live up to his financial obligations. Having a kid isn't cheap."

"I can handle it by myself."

"Vick . . . being a single parent isn't something I'd wish on anyone."

"The concept of parenting, in any form, freaks you out," Victoria had said. "Which is perfectly understandable, coming from our background. But I want this baby. And I'll do a good job."

And she had. Victoria had turned out to be a responsible parent, patient and kind with her only child, protective without being overcontrolling. God knew where such mothering skills had come from. They had to have been instinctive, since Victoria certainly hadn't learned them from her own parents.

Mark knew without a doubt that he didn't have those instincts. Which was why it was a shock upon shock when he learned that he had not only just lost a sister, he had gained a child.

Being named as Holly's guardian was nothing he

had ever anticipated. He knew his own capabilities about most things, and he had a good idea of what he probably would be able to do in situations he hadn't yet encountered. But this . . . taking care of a child . . . this was beyond him.

If Holly had been a boy, he might've had half a chance. Boys weren't all that hard to figure out. The entire female gender, on the other hand, was a mystery. Mark had long ago accepted that women were complicated. They said things like, "If you don't already know, I'm not going to tell you." They never ordered their own desserts, and when they asked your opinion on which outfit to wear, they always wore the one you didn't pick. Still, although Mark would never claim to understand women, he adored them: their elusiveness, the surprises of them, their intricate, fascinating shifts of mood.

But to *actually raise* one . . . Jesus, no. The stakes were too high. There was no way he could set a good enough example. And guiding a daughter through the treacherous, tricky climate of a society that presented every kind of pitfall . . . God knew he had no qualifications for that.

Mark and his siblings had been raised by parents whose version of marriage had been a war of attrition in which their children had been used as pawns. As a result, the three Nolan brothers— Mark, Sam, and Alex—had been fine with the idea of going their separate ways upon reaching adulthood. Victoria, on the other hand, had craved the kind of connection their family had never been able to muster. She had finally found it in Holly, and that had made her feel lucky.

But one wrong half turn of a steering wheel, one patch of wet road, one out-of-control moment, and the amount of life measured out to Victoria Nolan had run cruelly short.

Victoria had left a sealed letter, addressed to Mark, kept in a file with the will.

There's no other choice but you. Holly doesn't know Sam or Alex at all. I write this hoping that you'll never have to read it, but if you are . . . take care of my daughter, Mark. Help her. She needs you. I know how overwhelming this responsibility must seem. I'm sorry. I know you didn't ask for this. But you can do it. You'll figure everything out.

Just start by loving her. The rest will follow.

"You're really going to take her?" Sam had asked Mark on the day of the funeral, after a reception at Victoria's house. It had been eerie to see everything the way she'd left it: the books in the bookcase, a pair of shoes tossed carelessly to the closet floor, a tube of lip gloss on the bathroom counter.

"Of course I'm going to take her," Mark said. "What else can I do?"

12

"There's Alex. He's married. Why didn't Vick leave Holly to him and Darcy?"

Mark gave him a speaking glance. Their youngest brother's marriage was like a virus-ridden computer—you couldn't open it in safe mode, and it ran programs that seemed harmless but performed all kinds of malicious functions.

"Would *you* leave your kid to them?" he asked.

Slowly, Sam shook his head. "I guess not."

"So you and I are all Holly's got."

Sam gave him a wary look. "You're the one who's signing on for this, not me. There's a reason Vick didn't name me as her guardian. I'm not good with kids."

"You're still Holly's uncle."

"Yes, *uncle.* My responsibilities are limited to making jokes about body functions and drinking too much beer at family cookouts. I'm not the dad type."

"Neither am I," Mark said grimly. "But we have to try. Unless you want to sign her up for foster care."

Scowling, Sam rubbed his face with both hands. "What is Shelby's take on this?"

Mark shook his head at the mention of his girlfriend, an interior decorator he had met when she had been decorating the high-end house of a friend on Griffin Bay. "I've only been going out with her a couple of months. She'll either deal with it or bail—that's up to her. But I'm not going to ask her for help. This is my responsibility. And yours."

"Maybe I could babysit sometime. But don't count on much help; I've sunk everything I have into the vineyard."

"Exactly what I told you not to do, genius."

Sam's eyes, the same blue-green as his own, narrowed. "If I listened to your advice, I'd be making your mistakes instead of my own." He paused. "Where does Vick keep the booze?"

"Pantry." Mark went to a cabinet, found two glasses, and filled them with ice.

Sam rummaged through the pantry. "It feels weird, drinking her liquor when she's . . . gone."

"She'd be the first to tell us to go ahead."

"Probably right." Sam came to the table with a bottle of whiskey. "Did she have life insurance?"

Mark shook his head. "She let it lapse."

Sam shot him a look of concern. "Guess you're going to put the house up for sale?"

"Yeah. I doubt we'll get much for it in this market." Mark pushed a glass over to him. "Don't hold back," he said.

"Don't worry." Sam didn't stop pouring until both glasses were liberally filled.

They resumed their seats across from each other, raised their whiskey in a silent toast, and drank. It was good liquor, sliding smoothly down Mark's throat, sending a rush of mellow fire into his chest.

He found unexpected comfort in his brother's

presence. It seemed their cantankerous childhood history—the fights, the small betrayals—would no longer get in their way. They were adults now, with a potential for friendship that had never existed while their parents had still been alive.

With Alex, however, you could never get close enough to like or dislike him. Alex and his wife, Darcy, had come to the funeral, stayed at the reception for about fifteen minutes, and then left with hardly a word to anyone.

"They've gone already?" Mark had asked incredulously upon discovering their absence.

"If you wanted them to stay longer," Sam had said, "you should have held the funeral reception at Nordstrom."

No doubt people wondered how three brothers could reside on an island with approximately seven thousand residents and have so little to do with one another. Alex lived with Darcy in Roche Harbor on the north side. When he wasn't busy with his condo development, he was taking his wife to social events in Seattle. Mark, for his part, kept busy with a small coffee-roasting business he'd established in Friday Harbor. And Sam, who was always in his vineyard, tending and cosseting his vines, felt a deeper connection to nature than to people.

The only thing they all had in common was their love of San Juan Island. It was part of an archipelago that consisted of approximately two hundred islands, some of them encompassed by the Washington mainland counties of Whatcom and Skagit. The Nolans had spent their childhood in the rain shadow of the Olympic Mountains, a place sheltered from much of the grayness of the rest of the Pacific Northwest.

The Nolans had grown up breathing in humid ocean air, their bare feet constantly coated with the silt of exposed mudflats. They had been gifted with damp lavender mornings, dry blue days, and the most beautiful sunsets on earth. Nothing could compare to the sight of nimble sandpipers chasing the waves. Or of bald eagles swooping low and fast in pursuit of prey. Or of the dance of orcas, their sleek forms diving, spy-hopping, and cutting through the Salish Sea as they fed on the rich pulse of salmon runs.

The brothers had rambled over every inch of the island, up and down wind-bitten slopes above the seacoast, among somber columns of timber forests, and across meadows thick with orchard grasses and wildflowers with alluring names . . . Chocolate Lily, Shooting Star, Sea Blush. No mix of water, sand, and sky had ever been as perfectly proportioned.

Although they had gone off to college and tried living in other places, the island had always lured them back. Even Alex, with all his hard-shelled ambitions, had come back. It was the kind of life in which you knew the local farmers who grew most of the produce you ate, and the guy who made the soap you washed with, and you were on a first-name basis with the owners of the restaurants you went to. You could hitchhike safely, with friendly islanders giving one another a lift when they needed it.

Victoria had been the only one in the family who had ever found something worth leaving the island for. She had fallen in love with the glass peaks and cement valleys of Seattle, the urban coffee-and-culture scene, the stylishly understated restaurants that seduced your taste buds, the sensory labyrinth of Pike Place Market.

In response to a comment of Sam's that everyone did too much talking and thinking in the city, Victoria had replied that Seattle made her smarter.

"I don't need to be smarter," Sam had said. "The smarter you are, the more reasons you have to be miserable."

"That explains why we Nolans are always in such high spirits," Mark had told Victoria, making her laugh.

"Not Alex, though," she had said, sobering after a minute. "I don't think Alex has been happy a day in his life."

"Alex doesn't want happiness," Mark had replied. "He's fine with the substitutes."

Bringing his mind back to the present, Mark wondered what Victoria would say if she knew that

17

he was going to raise Holly on San Juan Island. He didn't realize he had given voice to the thought until Sam replied.

"Like she would have been surprised? Vick knew you'd never move away from the island. Your coffee business is there, your home, your friends. I'm sure she knew you'd take Holly to Friday Harbor, if anything happened to her."

Mark nodded, feeling hollow and bleak. The magnitude of the child's loss was not something he could dwell on for long.

"Did she say anything today?" Sam asked. "I didn't hear a peep out of her."

In the days since she had been told of her mother's death, Holly had been silent, only responding to questions by nodding or shaking her head. She wore a distant, dazed expression, having retreated to an inner world where no one could intrude. On the night of Victoria's death, Mark had gone straight from the hospital to her house, where a babysitter was looking after the little girl. He had broken the news to the child in the morning, and had stayed practically within arm's reach of her ever since.

"Nothing," Mark said. "If she doesn't start talking by tomorrow, I'm going to take her to the pediatrician." He let out a shallow, shaken breath before adding, "I don't even know who that is."

"There's a list on the fridge," Sam said. "It's got a few numbers on it, including one for Holly's doctor. I'm guessing Vick kept it there in case a babysitter needed it in an emergency."

Mark went to the refrigerator, pulled off a Post-it note, and stuck it in his wallet. "Great," he said sardonically. "Now I know at least as much as the babysitter."

"It's a start."

Returning to the table, Mark took a long, deliberate swallow of whiskey. "There's something I need to talk to you about. Living in my condo at Friday Harbor isn't going to work for me and Holly. There's only one bedroom, and no yard for her to play in."

"Are you going to sell it?"

"Rent it out, maybe."

"And then where would you go?"

Mark paused for a long, deliberate moment. "You've got plenty of room."

Sam's eyes widened. "No, I don't."

Two years earlier Sam had bought fifteen acres at False Bay in pursuit of his long-held dream to establish his own winery. The property, with its well-drained sand and gravel soil and cool-climate *terroir,* was perfect for a vineyard. Along with the land had come a cavernous dilapidated Victorian country farmhouse with a wrap-around porch, multiple bay windows, a big corner turret, and multicolored fish-scale shingles.

"Fixer-upper" was far too kind a term to use for the place, which was troubled by creaks, sags, weird drips, and puddles without apparent origin. Past residents had left their mark on the house, installing bathrooms where none had been intended, putting in flimsy chipwood walls, shallow closets with wobbly sliding pocket doors, slathering cherrywood shelves and moldings with cheap white paint. The original hardwood floors had been covered with linoleum or shag carpeting you could actually lie on and make rug angels.

But the house had three things going for it: there was more than enough room for two bachelors and a six-year-old kid, there was a big yard and orchard, and its location on False Bay was Mark's favorite part of the island.

"It's not happening," Sam said flatly. "I like living alone."

"What do you have to lose by letting us stay with you? There's not a single aspect of your life that we would interfere with." *We. Us.* Pronouns that were apparently going to be replacing the "I" in most of Mark's sentences from now on.

"You're kidding, right? Do you know what life is like for single guys with kids? You miss out on all the hot women, because none of them wants to get conned into babysitting, and they don't want to raise someone else's kid. Even if by some miracle of God you manage to get a hot woman, you can't keep her. No spontaneous weekends in Portland or Vancouver, no wild sex, no sleeping late, *ever.*"

"You don't do that stuff now," Mark pointed out. "You spend all your time in the vineyard."

"The point is, that's my choice. But there's no choice when there's a kid. While your friends are knocking back a beer and watching a game, you're at the grocery store looking for stain-fighting liquids and Goldfish crackers."

"It's not forever."

"No, just the rest of my youth." Sam lowered his head to the table as if to pound it, then settled for resting it on a forearm.

"How are you defining your youth, Sam? Because from where I'm sitting, your youth jumped the shark a couple years back."

Sam stayed motionless except for the middle finger that shot up from his right hand. "I had plans for my thirties," he said in a muffled voice. "And none of them included kids."

"Neither did mine."

"I'm not ready for this."

"Neither am I. That's why I need your help." Mark let out a taut sigh. "Sam, when have I ever asked you for anything?"

"Never. But do you have to start now?"

Mark made his tone quietly persuasive. "Think of it this way . . . we'll start off slow. We'll be Holly's tour guides to life. Easygoing tour guides who never come up with crap like 'reasonable punishments' or 'because I said so.' I've already accepted that I won't do the best job raising a kid

21

. . . but unlike our dad, my mistakes are going to be benign. I'm not going to backhand her when she doesn't clean up her room. I'm not going to make her eat celery if she doesn't like it. No mind games. Hopefully she'll end up with a decent worldview and a self-supporting job. God knows however we do this, it'll be better than sending her off to be raised by strangers. Or worse, our other relatives."

A few muttered curses emerged from the hard-muscled crucible of Sam's arms. As Mark had hoped, his brother's innate sense of fairness had gotten the better of him. "Okay." His back rose and fell with a sigh before he repeated, "Okay. But I have conditions. Starting with, I want the rent from your condo when you lease it out."

"Done."

"And I'll need your help fixing up the house."

Mark gave him a wary look. "I'm not great with home renovations. I can do the basics, but—"

"You're good enough. And the sight of you refinishing my floors will be a balm to my soul." Now that Sam had the promise of rent money and cheap labor, some of his hostility had faded. "We'll try it out for a couple of months. But if it's not working for me, you'll have to take the kid somewhere else."

"Six months."

"Four."

"Six."

"All right, damn it. Six months." Sam poured more whiskey. "My God," he muttered. "Three Nolans under one roof. A disaster waiting to happen."

"The disaster's already happened," Mark said curtly, and would have said more, but he heard a soft shuffling sound in the hallway.

Holly came to the kitchen doorway. She'd gotten out of bed and was standing there with a bewildered, sleep-dazed expression. A small refugee, dressed in pink pajamas, her feet pale and vulnerable on the dark slate floor.

"What's the matter, honey?" Mark asked gently, going to her. He picked her up—she couldn't have weighed more than forty pounds—and she clung to him like a monkey. "Can't sleep?" The round weight of her head on his shoulder, the soft tangled mass of her blond hair, the little-girl smell of crayons and strawberry shampoo filled him with unnerving tenderness.

He was all she had.

Just start by loving her . . .

That would be the easy part. It was the rest of it he was worried about.

"I'm going to tuck you in, sugar-bee," Mark said. "You need to sleep. We've got a lot of busy days ahead of us."

Sam followed as Mark carried Holly back to her room. The four-poster bed was fitted with a frame at the top, from which Victoria had hung an assortment of fabric butterflies with sheer gauzy wings. Settling her on the mattress, Mark pulled the covers up to her chin, and sat on the edge of the bed. Holly was quiet and unblinking.

Looking into her haunting blue eyes, Mark smoothed the hair back from her forehead. He would have done anything for her. The force of his own emotions surprised him. He couldn't make up for what Holly had lost. He couldn't give her the life she would have had. But he would take care of her. He wouldn't abandon her.

All of those thoughts, and more, flooded his mind. But what he said was, "You want me to tell you a bedtime story?"

Holly nodded, her gaze flicking briefly to Sam, who had come to lean against the doorjamb.

"Once upon a time," Mark said, "there were three bears."

"Two uncle bears," Sam added from the doorway, sounding vaguely resigned, "and a baby bear."

Mark smiled faintly as he continued to smooth Holly's hair. "And they all lived in a big house by the sea . . ."

Two

. . . .

The bell on the shop door jingled as the man of Maggie's dreams walked in. Or more accurately, he was the man of someone else's reality, since he was holding the hand of a small girl who had to be his daughter. While the child hurried to look at a huge carousel that revolved slowly in the corner of the toy store, her father wandered in more slowly.

Low-slanting September sunlight passed over dark hair cut in short, efficient layers, the ends curling slightly against the back of his neck. As he passed a mobile dangling from the ceiling, he ducked his head to avoid colliding with it. He moved like an athlete, relaxed but alert, giving the impression that if you threw something at him unexpectedly, he'd catch it without hesitation.

Sensing Maggie's helpless interest, he glanced in her direction. He had strong-boned, rough-edged good looks, and eyes so blue you could see them from across the shop. Although he was tall and striking, there was no swagger in him . . . just quiet, potent confidence. With the beginnings of a five-o'clock shadow, and jeans worn to the point of raggedness, he was a little bit scruffy and a whole lot sexy.

And he was taken.

Tearing her gaze away from him, Maggie hastily

picked up a wooden weaving loom. With great care, she restrung a few stretchy fabric loops.

Shoving his hands in his pockets, the guy wandered to his daughter. He took an interest in the train that went around the entire store, the tracks positioned on a shelf built close to the ceiling.

Since the Magic Mirror had opened three months earlier, business had been brisk. Tables were piled with old-fashioned toys: binoculars, handmade yo-yos, wooden vehicles, lifelike stuffed animals, sturdy kites.

"That's Mark Nolan and his niece Holly," Elizabeth, one of the store clerks, murmured to Maggie. Elizabeth was a retiree who had taken a part-time job at the shop. She was a vivacious older woman who seemed to know everyone on San Juan Island. Maggie, having just moved from Bellingham at the beginning of the summer, had found Elizabeth to be an invaluable resource.

Elizabeth knew the customers, their family histories and personal tastes, and she remembered the names of everyone's grandchildren. "Isn't it getting close to Zachary's birthday?" she might ask a friend who was browsing through the shop. Or, "Heard poor little Madison's under the weather . . . we've got some new books, perfect for reading in bed." Whenever Elizabeth was there, no one left the Magic Mirror without buying something. Occasionally Elizabeth called customers when the store had something new in that she thought they'd like. When you lived on an island, word of mouth was still the most effective selling tool.

Maggie's eyes widened slightly. "His niece?"

"Yes, Mark's raising her. Her mother died in a car wreck about six months ago, poor little thing. So Mark brought her over from Seattle, and they've been living at Rainshadow Vineyard, at his brother Sam's house. I couldn't imagine those two trying to take care of a little girl by themselves, but they've managed so far."

"They're both single?" A question that Maggie had no business asking, but it slipped out before she could stop it.

Elizabeth nodded. "There's another brother, Alex, who is married, but I heard they're having trouble." She cast a regretful look at Holly. "She ought to have a woman in her life. I think it's one of the reasons she won't talk."

Maggie's brow furrowed. "To strangers, you mean?"

"To anyone. Not since the accident."

"Oh," Maggie whispered. "One of my nephews wouldn't talk to anyone at school when he started elementary school. But he would talk to his parents at home."

Elizabeth gave a regretful shake of her head. "As far as I know, Holly's quiet all the time." She set a pink cone hat with a veil over her white curls that danced like butterfly antennae, and adjusted an elastic band beneath her chin. "They're hoping she'll come out of it soon. The doctor told them not to push her."

Picking up a scepter topped with a sparkling star, Elizabeth went back to the party room, where a birthday celebration was in progress. "Time for cake, Your Majesties!" she announced, and was greeted with high-pitched squeals before the door closed behind her.

After ringing up a customer who had bought a stuffed rabbit and a picture book, Maggie glanced around the shop until she found Holly Nolan again.

The child was staring at a fairy house that had been fastened to the wall. Maggie had made it herself, decorating the roof with dried moss and gold-painted bottle caps. The circular door had been made from the casing of a broken pocket watch. Standing on her toes, Holly squinted through a tiny window.

Emerging from behind the counter, Maggie approached her, not missing the subtle stiffening of the child's back.

"Do you know what that is?" Maggie asked gently.

Holly shook her head, not sparing her a glance.

"Most people think it's a dollhouse, but it's not. It's a fairy house."

Holly looked at her then, her gaze traveling from Maggie's lo-top Converse sneakers all the way to her curly red hair.

Maggie felt an unexpected rush of tenderness as they studied each other. She saw the frail solemnity of a child who no longer trusted in the permanence of anything. And yet she sensed Holly still inhabited the corners of her childhood, ready to be tempted by something that hinted of magic.

"The fairy who lives here is always gone in the daytime," Maggie said. "But she comes back at night. I'm sure she wouldn't mind if I gave you a peek into her house. Would you like to see it?"

Holly nodded.

Carefully, Maggie reached for the clasp at the side of the house and unfastened it. The entire front swung open to reveal three small furnished rooms containing a bed made of twigs . . . a gilded espresso cup for a bathtub . . . a table shaped like a mushroom, with a wine cork for a chair.

Maggie was gratified to see a hesitant smile spread across Holly's face, revealing the endearing gap of a missing tooth on the bottom row. "She doesn't have a name, this fairy," Maggie said confidentially, closing the front of the house. "Not a human name, that is. Only a fairy name, which of course humans could never pronounce. So I've been trying to think of what to call her. When I decide, I'll paint it over the front door. Lavender, maybe. Or Rose. Do you like either of those?"

Holly shook her head and bit her lip, regarding the house pensively.

"If you have a name in mind," Maggie told her, "you can write it down for me."

They were joined by Holly's uncle, a protective hand closing over one frail shoulder. "Everything okay, Holly?"

An attractive voice, dark and slow-simmered. But there was a gleam of warning in the glance he shot at Maggie. She fell back a step as she found herself confronted by six-foot-plus of uncompromising male. Mark Nolan wasn't precisely handsome, but his bold features and dark good looks made handsomeness irrelevant. A small crescent-shaped scar high on his cheek, faintly silvered in the light from the window, gave him an agreeable hint of toughness. And the eyes . . . a rare shade of blue-green, like the ocean in a tropical travel brochure. He seemed dangerous in some way that had yet to reveal itself. He was the mistake you would never entirely regret making.

She managed a neutral smile. "Hi. I'm Maggie Conroy. This is my shop."

Nolan didn't bother to volunteer his own name. Noticing his niece's fascination with the fairy house, he asked, "Is that for sale?"

"Afraid not. It's part of the shop decor." Glancing down at Holly, Maggie added, "They're not hard to make. If you draw a picture of one and bring it to me, I could help you build it." Lowering to sit on her heels, she looked directly into the girl's small face. "You never know if a fairy will come to live in it. All you can do is wait, and cross your fingers."

"I don't think—" Mark Nolan began, but he fell abruptly silent when Holly smiled and reached out to touch one of the crystal earrings that dangled from Maggie's ears, sending the weight of it swinging.

Something about the girl, with her off-center ponytail and wistful gaze, reached past several layers of self-protection. Maggie felt a sweet, almost painful ache in her chest as they contemplated each other.

I understand, Maggie wanted to tell her. *I've lost someone, too.* And there were no rules for how to deal with the death of someone you loved. You had to accept that the loss would always stay with you, like a reminder note pinned to the inside of your jacket. But there were still opportunities for happiness. Even joy. Maggie couldn't let herself doubt that.

"Would you like to see a book about fairies?" she asked, and saw eagerness light up the girl's face.

As Maggie stood, she felt the brush of Holly's hand against hers. Her hand closed carefully over the cool little bundle of fingers.

Risking a glance at Mark Nolan, Maggie saw that his face had gone blank, his unfriendly gaze arrowing to their clasped hands. She sensed that it had surprised him, this willingness of Holly's to hold hands with a stranger. When he made no objection, Maggie drew Holly along with her toward the back of the store.

"The . . . the book section is over here," Maggie said. They reached a child-sized table and a pair of small chairs. While Holly sat, Maggie pulled a ponderous and richly colored volume from the bookshelves. "Here we are," she said brightly. "Everything you ever wanted to know about fairies." It was a beautifully illustrated book with several pages of pop-up scenes. Sitting on the tiny chair next to Holly's, Maggie opened the book for her.

Nolan stood nearby, appearing to check messages on his cell phone, but Maggie was aware of his covert interest. Although he was willing to let her interact with his niece, it wouldn't happen without his supervision.

Maggie and Holly looked at the section titled "What Fairies Do All Day," showing them stitching together rainbows like long ribbons, pruning their gardens, and having tea parties with butterflies and ladybugs.

From the corner of her eye, Maggie saw that Mark Nolan had pulled one of the sealed copies of the book from the shelf, and had put it in a handbasket. She couldn't help noticing the hard, lean lines of his body, the flex of muscle beneath ancient denim and a worn gray T-shirt.

Whatever Nolan did for a living, he dressed like a working-class guy, with worn shoes, Levi's, and a decent but unspectacular watch. That was one of the things Maggie liked about the islanders, or Sanjuaneros, as they lightly referred to themselves. You could never tell who was a millionaire and who was a landscaper.

An elderly woman approached the register, and Maggie pushed the book a bit closer to Holly. "I have to go help someone," she said. "You can look at that book as long as you want."

Holly nodded, gently tracing the edge of a pop-up rainbow with her fingertip.

Going behind the counter, Maggie faced a woman with artfully styled gray hair and thick-lensed glasses.

"I'd like this gift-wrapped, please," the woman said, pushing a boxed wooden train set across the counter.

"This is a great starter set," Maggie told her. "You can rearrange the track four different ways. And later on, you can add the swivel bridge. It has little gates that automatically open and close."

"Really? Maybe I should get one of them right now."

"Let me show one to you. We've got it on display near the front. . . ." As Maggie guided the woman to the train table, she saw that Holly and her uncle had left the book area and were browsing among racks of fairy wings on the wall. Nolan lifted the child to give her a better view of the higher-up wings. Maggie's stomach did a funny little swoop as she saw how his T-shirt molded to the powerful line of his back.

Dragging her gaze away from him, Maggie turned her attention to gift-wrapping the train set. While Maggie worked, the customer squinted at a phrase painted on the wall behind the counter. *There's no sensation to compare with this . . . suspended animation, a state of bliss . . .*

"What a nice quote," the woman said. "Is it from a poem?"

"Pink Floyd," Nolan said as he came up to set a heavily filled handbasket on the counter. "It's from a song called 'Learning to Fly.'"

As Maggie met his gaze, she felt color blooming from head to toe. "You like Pink Floyd?"

He smiled slightly. "I did in high school. During a phase of wearing black and whining about my emotional isolation."

"I remember that phase," the elderly woman said. "Your parents wanted to call the governor and enlist you in the National Guard."

"Thank God they loved their country too much to go through with it." Nolan's smile widened, leaving Maggie momentarily dazzled, even though he hadn't been looking in her direction.

She fumbled a little as she slid the wrapped present into a bag with cord handles. "Here you go," she said brightly, nudging the bag toward the elderly woman.

Nolan reached for it. "That looks heavy, Mrs.

34

Borowitz. Why don't you let me carry it out to the car for you?"

The diminutive woman beamed at him. "Thank you, but I can manage. How are those brothers of yours?"

"Sam's great. Out in the vineyard most of the time. As for Alex . . . I haven't seen much of him lately."

"He's certainly putting his mark on Roche Harbor."

"Yeah." There was a wry twist to his mouth. "He won't rest until he's covered most of the island with condos and parking lots."

The woman looked down at Holly. "Hello, sweetheart. How are you?"

The child nodded bashfully and said nothing.

"You just started first grade, didn't you? Do you like your teacher?"

Another timid nod.

Mrs. Borowitz clucked gently. "Still not talking? Well, you need to start soon. How will anyone know what you're thinking if you don't tell them?"

Holly stared fixedly at the ground.

Although the words had not been meant unkindly, Maggie saw Nolan's jaw tighten.

"She'll get around to it," he said in a casual tone. "Mrs. Borowitz, that bag is bigger than you are. You're going to have to let me take it out for you, or they'll take back my merit badge."

The elderly woman chuckled. "Mark Nolan, I

know for a fact that you never earned a merit badge."

"That's because you never let me help you. . . ."

The pair bickered amiably as Nolan took the package from her and walked her to the door. He glanced back over his shoulder. "Holly, wait there for me. I'll be back in a second."

"She's fine here," Maggie said. "I'll look out for her."

Nolan's gaze slid to her briefly. "Thanks," he said, and left the shop.

Maggie let out a pent-up breath, feeling a little like she had just gotten off an amusement-park ride, her insides settling after having been rearranged.

Leaning against the counter, Maggie regarded Holly thoughtfully. The child's face was guarded, her eyes bright but opaque, like sea glass. Maggie tried to remember more about when her nephew, Aidan, hadn't been able to speak at school. Selective mutism, it was called. People often thought such behavior was willful or deliberate, but it wasn't. Aidan had gotten better in time, eventually responding to the patient overtures of his family and teacher.

"Do you know who you remind me of?" Maggie asked in a conversational tone. "The little mermaid. You've seen that movie, right?" Turning, she rummaged beneath the counter and found a large pink conch shell, part of a beach-themed display they had planned to put in the window soon. "I have something for you. A present." Coming around the counter, she held it up for Holly's inspection. "I know, it looks pretty ordinary. But there's something special about this shell. You can hear the ocean if you put it against your ear." She handed the conch over, and Holly held it carefully up to her ear. "Can you hear it?"

The child responded with a matter-of-fact shrug. Clearly the ocean-in-the-seashell trick was old news.

"Do you know *why* you can hear it?" Maggie asked.

Holly shook her head, looking intrigued.

"Some people—very practical, scientific people —say that the shell captures outside noise and lets it resonate inside the shell. However, other people"—Maggie gestured to herself and gave the girl a significant glance—"believe there's a little magic in it."

After considering this, Holly returned her meaningful glance and touched her own small chest.

Maggie smiled. "I have an idea. Why don't you take this shell home with you and practice making noise in it? You could sing or hum into it like this. . . ." She sent a wordless tune into the empty shell. "And someday maybe it could help your voice to come back. Just like the little mermaid."

Holly reached out and took the shell with both hands.

At that moment, the door opened, and Mark Nolan walked back into the store. His gaze went to Holly, who was staring intently into the aperture of the conch. He froze as he heard the girl begin to croon a few soft notes into the shell. His face changed. And in that one unguarded moment, Maggie saw a flashing succession of emotions: concern, fear, hope.

"What are you doing, Holls?" he asked casually, approaching them.

The girl paused and showed him the conch.

"It's a magic shell," Maggie said. "I told Holly she could take it home with her."

Nolan's dark brows lowered, and a shadow of annoyance crossed his face. "It's a nice conch," he told his niece. "But there's nothing magical about it."

"Oh, yes, there is," Maggie said. "Sometimes the most ordinary-looking things have magic in them . . . you just have to look hard enough."

A humorless smile touched Nolan's lips. "Right," he said darkly. "Thanks."

Too late, Maggie understood that he was one of those people who didn't encourage flights of fancy in their children. Heaven knew he was not alone. More than a few parents believed that children were better off with a strict diet of reality, rather than being confused by stories of made-up

38

creatures, or talking animals, or Santa Claus. In Maggie's opinion, though, fantasy allowed children to play with ideas, to find comfort and inspiration. However, it wasn't up to her to decide such things for someone else's child.

Abashed, Maggie retreated behind the counter and busied herself with ringing up the items in the basket: the fairy book, a puzzle, a jump rope with wooden handles, and a fairy ornament with iridescent wings.

Holly wandered away from the counter, humming softly into the conch. Nolan stared after his niece, then turned his attention back to Maggie. He spoke in an edgy undertone. "No offense, but—"

Which was the way people always started a sentence that ended up being offensive.

"—I prefer to be honest with kids, Miss . . ."

"Mrs.," Maggie said. "Conroy. And I prefer to be honest, too."

"Then why did you tell her that's a magic shell? Or that a fairy lives in that house on the wall?"

Maggie frowned as she tore the receipt from the register. "Imagination. Play. You don't know much about children, do you?"

It was instantly apparent that the shot had hit its target far harder than she had intended. Nolan's expression didn't change, but she saw a band of color burnish the crests of his cheeks and the bridge of his nose. "I became Holly's guardian about six months ago. I'm still learning. But one of my rules is not to let her believe in stuff that's not real."

"I'm sorry," she said sincerely. "I didn't mean to offend you. But just because you can't see something doesn't mean it's not real." She gave him an apologetic smile. "Do you want your receipt with you, or in the bag?"

Those mesmerizing eyes stared right into hers with an intensity that caused her brain to do an abrupt control-alt-delete. "In the bag." They were close enough that his scent reached her, an amazingly good smell of old-fashioned white soap, and sea salt, and a hint of coffee. Slowly he extended a hand across the counter. "Mark Nolan."

His grip was strong, his hand warm and work-roughened. It awakened a subtle pang of awareness that started deep in the pit of her stomach.

To Maggie's relief, the shop door jingled as someone else came in. Instantly she tugged her hand free. "Hello," she called out with artificial cheer. "Welcome to the Magic Mirror."

Nolan—Mark—was still staring at her. "Where are you from?"

"Bellingham."

"Why'd you move to Friday Harbor?"

"It seemed like the right place for the shop." Maggie gave him a little shrug, to indicate that there was too much to explain. That didn't appear to dissuade him. The questions were gentle but persistent, nipping at the heels of her every answer.

"You got family here?"

"No."

"Then you must have followed a guy."

"No, I . . . why do you say that?"

"When a woman like you moves here, there's usually a guy."

She shook her head. "I'm a widow."

"I'm sorry." His steady gaze kindled a hot, shaky feeling inside, not entirely unpleasant. "How long ago?"

"Almost two years. I can't . . . I don't talk about it."

"An accident?"

"Cancer." She was so aware of him, the healthy masculine vitality of him, that she was covered with a full-bodied flush. It had been a long time since she'd felt this kind of attraction, extravagant in its intensity, and she didn't know what to do with it. "I have friends who live at Smugglers Cove, on the west side—"

"I know where it is."

"Oh. Of course, you grew up here. Well, my friend Ellen knew I wanted to make a new start somewhere, after my husband . . . after . . ."

"Ellen Scolari? Married to Brad?"

Maggie's brows lifted in surprise. "You know them?"

"There aren't many people on this island I don't

know." His eyes narrowed speculatively. "They haven't mentioned you. How long—"

A little whisper interrupted him.

"Uncle Mark."

"Just a minute, Holls, I'm—" Mark broke off and went very still. He did a near-comical double take, his stunned gaze falling to the child beside him. "Holly?" He sounded breathless.

The girl smiled up at him uncertainly. Standing on her toes, she reached over the counter to give the shell to Maggie. And she added in another hesitant but perfectly audible whisper, "Her name is Clover."

"The fairy?" Maggie asked in a hushed voice, while the hair on the back of her neck lifted. Holly nodded. Swallowing hard, Maggie managed to say, "Thank you for telling me, Holly."

Three

In the shock of hearing Holly's whisper, Mark forgot everything: their surroundings, the woman behind the counter. Six months they'd been trying to get Holly to say something, *anything*. Why it had happened here and now was something he'd parse out later with Sam. For now, he had to keep it together, to not overwhelm Holly with his reaction. It was just . . . *Christ.*

Mark couldn't stop himself from lowering to one knee and pulling Holly against him. Her fine-boned arms went around his neck. He heard himself saying her name in a shattered murmur. His eyes were stinging, and he was appalled to realize that he was on the verge of losing it.

But he couldn't control the tremors of relief at the evidence that Holly was apparently ready to start talking again. Maybe now he could let himself believe that she was going to be okay.

Feeling Holly wriggle to free herself from his tight grasp, Mark pressed a fervent kiss against her cheek and forced himself to let go. He stood, evaluated his emotion-clenched throat, and realized there was a good chance his voice would crack if he tried to say anything. He swallowed hard and blindly studied the Pink Floyd lyrics on the wall—not reading them, just focusing on the color of the paint, the texturing on the Sheetrock beneath.

Finally he slid a guarded look to the red-haired woman behind the counter—Maggie—who was holding the bag of stuff he'd just bought. He saw that she comprehended the significance of what had just happened.

He didn't know what to make of her. She was all of five foot two, with wild red curls that squiggled and zigzagged like hieroglyphs. Her figure was slender, dressed neatly in a white tee and jeans.

The face, half-hidden by those rampant curls, was pretty and fine-featured, her skin pale except for the fever-colored flush on her cheeks. And her eyes—dark and heavy-lashed, the color of bittersweet chocolate. She reminded him a little of the girls he used to know in college, the funny, interesting ones he would stay up half the night and talk with, but never date. He had dated the trophies instead, the ones that other guys had envied him for. It was only later that he had wondered what he might have missed out on.

"Can I talk to you sometime?" he asked, sounding more abrupt than he'd intended.

"I'm always here," Maggie said lightly. "Stop by whenever." She nudged the shell across the counter. "Why don't you take this home with you, Holly? Just in case you need it again."

"Hey, you guys!" A smooth, sunny voice came from behind Mark.

It was Shelby Daniels, Mark's girlfriend from

Seattle. She was smart, beautiful, and one of the nicest people Mark had ever known. You could take Shelby anywhere, in any kind of company, and she would find a way to fit in.

Shelby approached them, tucking a swing of gleaming blond hair behind one ear. She was dressed in khaki capris, a neat white shirt, and ballet flats, with no adornment other than single pearl earrings. "Sorry I was a few minutes late, you two. I had to try on something in the shop a couple doors down, but it didn't work out. I see you got some things, Holly."

The girl nodded, silent as usual.

With a mixture of worry and wry amusement, Mark realized Holly wasn't going to talk in front of Shelby. Should he say anything about what had just happened? No, that might put pressure on Holly. Best to leave it alone, stay loose.

Glancing at their surroundings, Shelby said, "What a great little shop. Next time I'm here, I'll have to pick up some things for my nephews. Christmas is going to be here before we know it." She curled her hand around Mark's arm and smiled up at him. "If I'm going to make the flight, we should probably go now."

"Sure thing." Mark took the bag from the counter, and reached for the shell in Holly's hand. "Want me to take that, Holls?"

She clutched it more tightly, wanting to carry it herself.

"Okay," Mark said, "but try not to drop it." Looking back at the little redhead behind the counter, he saw that she was reorganizing the pens in the cup by the register, straightening a row of tiny stuffed animals, busying herself with unnecessary tasks. Low-slanting light came through the windows and struck the brilliant red in her curls.

"Bye," he said. "And thanks."

Maggie Conroy gave him a cursory wave without really looking in his direction. Which was how he knew that she'd been set as thoroughly off balance as he had.

After dropping Shelby off at the airport, with its single strip of runway, Mark took Holly back home to Rainshadow Vineyard. It was about five and a half miles from Friday Harbor, on the southwest part of the island at False Bay. You had to drive with care on Sunday to avoid people on bicycles or horses. Black-tailed deer, tame as dogs, emerged from meadows of tall summer grass and blackberry bramble to saunter across the roads at their leisure.

Mark left the windows of his pickup open, letting the ocean-softened air flow into the vehicle. "Do you see that?" He pointed to a bald eagle soaring overhead.

"Uh-huh."

"Do you see what he's carrying in his talons?"

"A fish?"

"Probably. Either he pulled it from the water, or stole it from another bird."

"Where's he taking it?" Holly's voice was hesitant, as if she, too, was surprised to be hearing herself talk.

"Maybe to the nest. Male eagles take care of the chicks, just like the females do."

Holly received this information with a prosaic nod. From what she knew of the world, this was entirely plausible.

Mark had to force his hands to unclench from the steering wheel. Delight had filled him from head to toe. It had been so long since Holly had spoken, he'd actually forgotten the sound of her voice.

The child psychologist had said to start with nonverbal interactions, such as asking Holly to point to what she wanted on the menu, with the eventual goal of saying an actual word.

Until today, the only time Mark had ever gotten Holly to make a sound had been on a recent drive along Roche Harbor Road, when they had seen Mona the camel in her pasture. The camel, a well-known resident of the island, had been purchased from an exotic-animal dealer in Mill Creek, and brought to the island around eight or nine years ago. Feeling like an idiot, Mark had entertained Holly with imitation camel noises, and had been rewarded when Holly had briefly joined in.

"What helped you to find your voice,

sweetheart? Did it have something to do with Maggie? The red-haired woman?"

"It was the magic shell." Holly looked down at the conch, cradled tenderly in her small hands.

"But it's not—" Mark broke off. The point wasn't whether or not the conch was magic. The point was that the idea had connected with Holly, that it had been offered at just the right moment to help her find a way out of her silence. Magic, fairies . . . it was all part of some childhood lexicon he didn't know, some territory of imagination he had abandoned long ago. But Maggie Conroy hadn't.

He had never seen Holly connect with any woman like that, not Victoria's old friends, not her teacher, not even Shelby, with whom she'd spent a fair amount of time. Who was this Maggie Conroy? Why would a single young woman, still in her twenties, voluntarily move to an island where more than half the residents were over the age of forty-five? And why a toy store, for God's sake?

He wanted to see her again. He wanted to know everything about her.

The late Sunday afternoon light was honey colored and heavy, glazing the tidepools and shallow channels of False Bay. The habitat, about two hundred acres of sand flats, looked like an ordinary bay until it emptied completely at low tide. Gulls, herons, and eagles browsed amid the buffet of marine life on the sand flats: shore crabs,

48

worms, mud shrimp, bent-nose clams. You could walk out for at least a half mile in the rich silt before the tide came in.

The pickup turned onto the private graveled drive of Rainshadow Vineyard and approached the house. Outwardly, the place still looked worn and ramshackle, but inside they had been making structural repairs. The first thing Mark had done was fix Holly's bedroom, painting the walls robin's-egg blue and the trim creamy white. He'd brought over the furniture from her old bedroom, and had reattached the fabric butterflies to the poster bed.

The biggest project so far had been to create a bathroom decent enough for Holly. He and Sam had taken the walls down to the studs, installed new pipes, leveled out the floor, and put in a new bathtub, a high-tank toilet, and a marble-topped vanity. They let Holly choose the paint color once the walls had been Sheetrocked and plastered. Naturally she had chosen pink.

"It's period-appropriate," Mark said, reminding Sam that the color swatches had all come from a Victorian palette grouping.

"It's god-awful girly," Sam had said. "Every time I walk into that pink bathroom, I feel the need to do something manly afterward."

"Whatever that is, do it outside so we don't have to see you."

The next undertaking had been the kitchen,

where Mark had installed a brand-new stove with six burners, and a new refrigerator. He had proceeded to strip at least six coats of paint from the window and door framework, using an infrared paint remover and sander borrowed from Alex.

Alex had been unexpectedly generous with tools, supplies, and advice. In fact, he had started dropping by at least once a week, possibly because renovation and construction were his area of experience and his help was so obviously needed. In Alex's hands, scraps of useless wood could be turned into something clever and marvelous.

The second time he'd come to visit, Alex had built a set of cubbyholes in Holly's bedroom closet for her to store her shoes. To the little girl's delight, some of the cubbies had been set on a hidden hinge, swinging out to reveal a secret compartment. On another occasion, Alex brought over one of his construction crews when Mark and Sam discovered that some of the header beams on the front porch were buckling and crumbling like Styrofoam. Alex and the crew spent a day installing new supports, fixing damaged joists, and putting in new rain gutters. The job had been more than Mark and Sam could handle on their own, so they had sincerely appreciated the help. But knowing Alex . . .

"What do you think he wants?" Sam had asked Mark.

"For his niece not to be flattened by a collapsing house?"

"No, that would be attributing human motivations to him, and we agreed never to do that."

Mark tried, without success, to hold back a grin. Alex was so cool and emotionally distant that on occasion you had to question the existence of a pulse.

"Maybe he feels guilty for not having more to do with Vick before she died."

"Maybe's he's using any excuse to spend time away from Darcy. If I didn't already hate the idea of marriage so much, I sure would think twice about it after seeing Alex's."

"Obviously," Mark said, "a Nolan should never marry anyone who's too much like us."

"I think a Nolan should never marry anyone who'd have us."

Whatever the reason, Alex had continued to contribute to the restoration. As a result of their combined efforts, the house had begun to look better. Or at least like something normal people could live in.

"If you try to kick me out after all this," Mark had informed Sam, "you're going to end up buried in the backyard."

They both knew, however, that there was no chance Sam would ever kick them out. Because Sam, perhaps to his own surprise more than anyone else's, had taken to the child with instant devotion. Like Mark, he would have died for Holly if necessary. She got the best of everything they had.

At first cautious with her affection, Holly had quickly become attached to her uncles. Although they had gotten warnings from well-meaning outsiders not to spoil her, neither Sam nor Mark could see any evidence that their indulgence was doing any harm. In fact, both of them would have been happy to see a little more mischief from Holly. She was a good child, always doing what she was told.

When Holly wasn't in school, she accompanied Mark to his coffee-roasting site at Friday Harbor, watching the massive drum roaster heat raw arabica beans until their pale yellow skins caramelized to deep-gleaming brown. Sometimes he bought her ice cream at a shop near the harbor dock, and they would go "boat-shopping," browsing along rows of yachts, Nordic tugs, family cruisers, and crab boats with haystacked pots on the back decks.

Sam often took Holly out with him to tend the vines, or to hunt for starfish and sand dollars at low tide on False Bay. He wore pasta neckties she had made at school, and pinned her artwork on walls throughout the house.

"I had no idea what this was like," Sam had said one evening, carrying Holly into the house when she'd fallen asleep in the car. They had spent the afternoon at English Camp, the site where the British had lodged during joint occupation of the island until it had been awarded to the Americans. The national park, with its two miles of shoreline, was the perfect place to have a picnic and throw Frisbees. They had indulged in acrobatics to make Holly giggle, leaping to catch the Frisbee. They had brought her little tackle box and fishing rod, and Mark had taught her to cast for sea perch along the shore.

"What what's like?" Mark had opened the front door and flipped on the porch lights.

"Having a little kid around." Somewhat sheepishly, Sam clarified, "Having a little kid love you."

Holly's presence in their lives offered a kind of grace neither of them had ever known before. A reminder of innocence. Something happened to you, they discovered, when you were given the unconditional love and trust of a child.

You wanted to try to deserve it.

Mark and Holly went into the house through the kitchen, setting the packages and the conch on the table in the old-fashioned corner breakfast nook with built-in benches. They found Sam in the parlor, a painfully bare room with uncovered Sheetrock walls and a fractured chimney temporarily encased in steel mesh.

Sam was at the fireplace, building a frame for a soon-to-be-poured cement slab to support a new hearthstone. "This is going to be a son of a gun to fix," he said, in the middle of taking measurements. "I have to figure out how we can use the same chimney to vent two different fireplaces. This one leads directly to the upstairs bedroom, can you believe that?"

Leaning down, Mark murmured to Holly, "Go ask him what's for dinner."

The child obeyed, going to Sam's side and putting her mouth close to his ear. She whispered something and retreated a few steps.

Mark saw Sam go very still.

"You're talking," Sam said, turning slowly to look at the little girl. A questioning note had tipped his husky voice.

Holly shook her head, looking grave.

"Yes, you are, you just said something."

"No, I didn't." A titter escaped her as she saw Sam's expression.

"You did it again, by God! Say my name. Say it."

"Uncle Herbert."

Sam let out a breathless laugh and grabbed her, pulling her against his chest. "*Herbert?* Oh, now it's going to be chicken lips and lizard feet for dinner." Still clasping Holly, he looked at Mark with a wondering shake of his head, his color high, his eyes containing a suspicious glitter. *"How?"* was all he could manage to ask.

"Later," Mark said, and smiled.

"So what happened?" Sam asked, stirring a pot of spaghetti sauce on the stove. Holly was busy in the next room with her new puzzle. "How did you do it?"

Mark uncapped a beer and tilted the bottle back. "Wasn't me," he said after a biting-cold swallow. "We were in that toy shop on Spring Street, the new one, and there was this cute little redhead behind the counter. I've never seen her before—"

"I know who she is. Maggie something. Conner, Carter . . ."

"Conroy. You've met her?"

"No, but Scolari's been trying to get me to go out with her."

"He never mentioned her to me," Mark said, instantly offended.

"You're going out with Shelby."

"Shelby and I aren't exclusive."

"Scolari thinks Maggie's my type. We're closer in age. So she's cute? That's good. I thought I'd check her out before committing to anything—"

"I'm only two years older than you," Mark said in outrage.

Setting down the spoon, Sam picked up a glass of wine. "Did you ask her out?"

"No. Shelby was with me, and besides—"

"I call dibs."

"You don't get dibs on this one," Mark said curtly.

Sam's brows lifted. "You've already got a girlfriend. Dibs automatically go to the guy with the longest dry spell."

Mark's shoulders hitched in an irritable shrug.

"So what did Maggie do?" Sam pressed. "How did she get Holly to talk?"

Mark told him about the scene in the toy shop, about the magic shell, and how the suggestion of make-believe had worked a miracle.

"Amazing," Sam said. "I never would have thought of trying something like that."

"It was a matter of timing. Holly was finally ready to talk, and Maggie gave her a way to do it."

"Yeah, but . . . is it possible Holly would have started talking weeks ago if you or I had just figured it out?"

"Who knows? What are you getting at?"

Sam kept his voice low. "Do you ever think about what it's going to be like when she gets older? When she starts needing to talk to someone about girl stuff? I mean, who are we going to get to handle all that?"

"She's only six, Sam. Let's worry about it later."

"I'm worried that later's going to get here sooner than we think. I—" Sam broke off and rubbed his forehead as if to soothe away an oncoming headache. "I've got something to show you after Holly goes to bed."

"What? Should I be worried about something?"

"I don't know."

"Damn it, tell me now."

Sam kept his voice low. "Okay, I was going through Holly's homework folder to make sure she'd finished that coloring page . . . and I found

56

this." He went to a stack of paper on the counter and pulled out a single page. "The teacher gave them a writing prompt in class this week," he said. "A letter to Santa. And this is what Holly came up with."

Mark gave him a blank look. "A letter to Santa? We're still in the middle of September."

"They've already started running holiday commercials. And when I was at the hardware store yesterday, Chuck mentioned they were going to put out Christmas trees by the end of the month."

"Before Thanksgiving? Before *Halloween*?"

"Yes. All part of an evil worldwide corporate marketing plan. Don't try to fight it." Sam handed him the sheet of paper. "Take a look at this."

Dear Santa

I want just one thing this year
A mom
Plese dont forget I live in friday
harbor now.
thank you

love
Holly

Mark was silent for a full half minute.

"A mom," Sam said.

"Yeah, I get it." Still staring at the letter, Mark muttered, "What a hell of a stocking stuffer."

After dinner, Mark went out to the front porch with a beer and sat in a comfortably beat-up wooden chair. Sam was tucking Holly in and reading her a story from the book bought earlier that day.

It was still the time of year when sunsets were long and slow to fade, painting the sky over the bay in saturated pinks and oranges. Watching the shallows glitter between the brackets of deep-rooted madrone trees, Mark wondered bleakly what he was going to do about Holly.

A mom.

Of course that was what she wanted. No matter how Mark and Sam tried, there were some things they couldn't do for her. And although there were countless single dads who were raising daughters, no one could deny that there were milestones that a girl wanted a mother for.

Following the child psychologist's advice, Mark had set out a couple of framed pictures of Victoria. He and Sam made certain to talk about Victoria to Holly, to give the child a sense of connection with her mother. But Mark could do more than that, and he knew it. There was no reason Holly had to navigate the rest of her childhood without someone to mother her. Shelby was as close to perfect as it got. And Shelby had made it clear that despite Mark's ambivalence about marriage, she was willing to be patient. "Our marriage wouldn't be like your parents' marriage," she had pointed out gently. "It would be *ours*."

Mark had understood the point, even agreed. He knew he wasn't like his father, who had thought nothing of backhanding his children. Theirs had been a tempestuous household, filled to the roof with caterwauling, violence, drama. The Nolan parents' version of love, with its screaming fights and lurid reconciliations, had featured all the worst components of marriage, and none of its graces.

Understanding that even though his parents' marriage had been a perfect disaster, it didn't have to be that way, Mark had tried to remain neutral on the concept. He had always thought that when or if he ever found the right person, there would be some kind of inner confirmation, a sanction of the heart that would remove all doubt. So far that hadn't happened with Shelby.

What if it never happened with anyone? He tried to think of marriage as a pragmatic arrangement with someone you cared about. Maybe that was the best way to approach it, especially when you had a child's interests to consider. Shelby had the kind of personality—calm, pleasant, affectionate—that would make her a great mother.

Mark didn't believe in the illusions of romance, or of soul mates. He was the first to admit that he had an earthbound mind, anchored in cold, hard reality. He liked it that way. Was it unfair to Shelby to offer marriage based on practical considerations? Maybe not, as long as he was honest about his feelings—or lack of them.

Finishing his beer, he went back into the house, tossed the bottle into the recycling bin, and went to Holly's room. Sam had tucked her in and left the night-light on.

Holly's eyes were heavy-lidded, her small mouth twisting in a yawn. A teddy bear had been tucked in beside her, its bright button eyes regarding Mark expectantly.

Staring down at the little girl, Mark experienced one of those moments when you had a sudden and intense awareness of who you had been not all that long ago, and discovered that you were now in a different place entirely. He leaned over to kiss her forehead, as he did every night. He felt her spindly arms go around his neck, and heard her say in a drowsy, dream-colored voice, "I love you. I love you." And, turning to her side, she snuggled her bear and went to sleep.

Mark stood there blinking, trying to absorb the impact. For the first time in his life he knew what it felt like to have his heart broken . . . not broken in a sad or romantic sense, but broken open. He had never known this before, the desire to surround another human being with perfect happiness.

He would find a mother for Holly, the perfect mother. He would build a circle of people for her.

Usually a child was the result of a family. In this case, however, a family was going to be the result of a child.

Four

The four major islands in the area—San Juan, Orcas, Lopez, and Shaw—were all accessible by Washington State Ferries. You could park your car on the ferry, go to an upper-deck seating area, and prop your feet up during the hour and a half it took to get from San Juan to Anacortes on the mainland. The water was calm and the views were spectacular in summer and through the autumn.

Maggie drove to the ferry terminal at Friday Harbor, after dropping her dog off at the local pet hotel. Although she could have taken a half-hour flight that went directly to Bellingham, she preferred the ferry to flying. She liked looking at seaside homes, the island coastlines, the occasional glimpses of dolphins or lazing sea lions. Often flocks of feeding cormorants could be seen along tidal rips, black as cracked pepper scattered from a grinder.

Since one of her sisters was going to pick her up at the Anacortes terminal, and she wouldn't need a car while staying with her family, Maggie boarded the ferry as a walk-on passenger. The vessel was a steel electric-class ferry capable of accommodating almost a thousand passengers and eighty-five vehicles, and traveling up to thirteen knots.

Carrying her canvas overnight bag, Maggie went to the enclosed part of the main passenger deck. She walked along one of the rows of broad benches flanking the large glass windows. The Friday morning ferry was full, with passengers headed to Seattle for appointments or weekend entertainment. She found a pair of benches that faced each other. One of them was occupied by a man wearing khakis and a navy polo shirt. He was engrossed in a newspaper, a few discarded sections beside him.

"Excuse me, is this . . ." Maggie began, her voice fading as he looked up at her.

Before she saw anything else, she saw his blue-green eyes. She felt a hot jolt, as if her heart had been attached to jumper cables.

It was Mark Nolan . . . clean-shaven, well dressed, sexy in his unvarnished masculinity. Focusing on her, he set aside the paper and rose to his feet, an old-fashioned gesture that disconcerted her even further. "Maggie. Are you going to Seattle?"

"Bellingham." She damned herself for sounding breathless. "To visit my family."

He gestured to the bench opposite his. "Have a seat."

"Oh, I . . ." Maggie shook her head and cast a quick glance at their surroundings. "I wouldn't want to disturb your privacy."

"It's okay."

"Thank you, but . . . I don't want to do the airplane thing with you."

His dark brows lifted. "The airplane thing?"

"Yes, when I sit next to a stranger on an airplane, I sometimes end up telling him—or her—stuff I'd never admit even to my closest friends. But I never have to regret it, because I never see that person again."

"This isn't an airplane."

"But it *is* transportation."

Mark Nolan stood there staring down at her with a disarming glint of amusement in his eyes. "The ferry ride's not all that long. How much could you spill about yourself?"

"My entire life story."

He struggled with a smile, as if he didn't have many to spare. "Let's take our chances. Sit with me, Maggie."

A command rather than an invitation. But she found herself obeying. Setting her weekend bag on the floor, she took the bench opposite his. As she straightened, she noticed his gaze moving over her in a quick, efficient sweep. She was dressed in slim jeans, a white T-shirt, and a cropped black jacket.

"You look different," he said.

"It's my hair." Self-consciously, Maggie combed her fingers through a few long, straight locks. "I flat-iron it whenever I go to visit my family. Otherwise my brothers make fun of it, tug it . . . I'm the only one in the family with curly hair. I'm just

praying it doesn't rain. As soon as it gets wet—"
She made a gesture that mimicked an explosion.

"I like it both ways." The compliment was
delivered with a grave sincerity that Maggie
found a thousand times more charming than
flirtatiousness.

"Thank you. How's Holly?"

"Still talking. More all the time." He paused. "I
didn't have the chance to thank you the other day.
What you did for Holly . . ."

"Oh, it was nothing. I mean, I didn't really do
anything."

"It meant a lot to us." His gaze locked on hers.
"What are you and your family doing this
weekend?"

"We're just going to hang out. Cook, eat, drink
. . . my parents have a big old house in Edgemoor,
and about a million grandchildren. I have seven
brothers and sisters."

"You're the youngest," he said.

"Second youngest." She gave a disconcerted
laugh. "Close enough. How did you guess?"

"You're outgoing. You smile a lot."

"What are you? Oldest? Middle?"

"Oldest."

Maggie studied him frankly. "Which means you
like to make the rules, you're dependable . . . but
sometimes you can be a know-it-all."

"I'm right most of the time," he admitted
modestly.

A laugh rustled in her throat.

"Why did you open a toy store on the island?" he asked.

"It was sort of a natural segue. I used to paint children's furniture. That was how I met my husband. He had an unfinished furniture factory where I bought some of my stuff—little table-and-chair sets, bed frames—but after we got married I stopped painting for a while, because of his . . . you know, the cancer. And when I started working again, I wanted to try something different. Something fun."

When she saw that he was about to ask something else, possibly about Eddie, she forestalled him by asking quickly, "What do you do?"

"I have a coffee-roasting business."

"Like a home-based business, or—"

"I've got two partners, and a facility in Friday Harbor. We have a big industrial roaster that can produce about a hundred pounds per hour. We have about a half-dozen roast profiles we sell under our own name, but we've also come up with a few different lines for outlets on the island as well as Seattle, Lynnwood . . . and a restaurant in Bellingham, actually."

"Really? What's the name?"

"A vegetarian place called Garden Variety."

"I love that place! But I've never tried the coffee."

"Why not?"

"I gave it up a few years ago, after reading an article that said it wasn't good for you."

"It's practically a health tonic," Mark said indignantly. "Full of antioxidants and phyto-chemicals. It reduces your risk of certain kinds of cancer. Did you know that the word 'coffee' comes from an Arabic phrase that translates to 'wine of the bean'?"

"I didn't know that," Maggie said, smiling. "You take your coffee seriously, don't you?"

"Every morning," he replied, "I run to the coffeemaker like a soldier returning to a lost love after the war."

Maggie grinned, thinking what a wonderful voice he had, low but penetrating. "When did you start drinking it?"

"High school. I was studying for an exam. I tried my first cup of coffee because I thought it would help me stay awake."

"What do you like most about it? The taste? The caffeine?"

"I like starting the day with news and Jamaica Blue Mountain. I like having a cup in the afternoon while complaining about the Mariners or the Seahawks. I like knowing that in one cup of coffee, you're getting flavors from places most of us will never see. The Tanzanian foothills of Kilimanjaro . . . the Indonesian islands . . . Colombia, Ethiopia, Brazil, Cameroon . . . I like it that a truck driver can have just as good a cup of coffee as a millionaire. But most of all I like the ritual. It brings friends together, it's the perfect ending to dinner . . . and on occasion it can tempt a beautiful woman to come up to your apartment."

"That has nothing to do with coffee. You could tempt a woman with a glass of tap water." An instant later, eyes widening, Maggie covered her mouth with her hand. "I don't know why I said that," she said through the screen of her fingers, mortified and marveling.

Their gazes met for an electric moment. And then a smile touched his lips, and Maggie felt her heart give a hard extra thump.

Mark shook his head to indicate that it was no problem. "I was forewarned." He gestured to their surroundings. "Transportation makes you lose your inhibitions."

"Yes." Mesmerized by his warm blue-green eyes, Maggie struggled to regain the thread of conversation. "What were we talking about? . . . Oh, coffee. I've never had coffee that tasted as good as the roasted beans smell."

"Someday I'll make you the best cup of coffee you've ever had. You'll follow me around begging for more hot water percolated through ground robusta."

As Maggie laughed, she sensed that something had come alive in the air around them. Attraction, she realized in wonder. She had thought somehow that she'd lost the capacity for this, the vibrant sensual awareness of another person.

The ferry was moving. She hadn't even noticed the blare of the ferry horn. The powerful engine sent vibrations along the bones of the vessel, softer thrums milling through the floors and seats, as regular as a heartbeat.

Maggie thought she should take an interest in the view as they headed across the strait, but it had lost its usual power to entice her. She looked back at the man opposite her, the relaxed strength of him, the splayed knees and the long arm propped on the back of the bench.

"How are you spending the weekend?" she asked.

"Visiting a friend."

"The woman who was at the store with you?"

His expression became guarded. "Yes. Shelby."

"She seemed nice."

"She is."

Maggie knew she should have left it at that. But her curiosity about him was growing beyond all casual boundaries. As she tried to summon an image of the composed, attractive blond woman— Shelby—she remembered having thought that they looked right together. Like the couples in jewelry commercials. "Is it serious between you?"

He pondered that. "I don't know."

"How long have you been going out?"

"A few months." A contemplative pause before he added, "Since January."

"Then you already know if things are serious."

Mark looked torn between annoyance and amusement. "It takes some of us longer to figure it out than others."

"What's left to figure out?"

"If I can overcome the fear of eternity."

"I should tell you my motto. It's a quote from Emily Dickinson."

"I don't have a motto," he said reflectively.

"Everyone should have a motto. You can borrow mine if you want."

"What is it?"

" 'Forever is composed of nows.' " Maggie paused, her smile turning wistful at the edges. "You shouldn't worry about forever . . . time runs out faster than you expect."

"Yes." Somewhere in his quiet tone there was a bleak note. "I found that out when I lost my sister."

She gave him a sympathetic glance. "You were close to her?"

There was an unaccountably long pause. "The Nolans have never been what anyone would call a close-knit family. It's like a casserole. You can take a bunch of ingredients that are fine on their own, but put them all together and it turns into something really terrible."

"Not all casseroles are bad," Maggie said.

"Name a good one."

"Macaroni and cheese."

"That's not a casserole."

"What is it, then?"

"It's a vegetable."

Maggie burst out laughing. "Good try. But it is a casserole."

"If you say so. But it's the only casserole I like. All the others taste like something you put together to empty out the pantry."

"I have my grandmother's recipe for mac and cheese. Four kinds of cheese. And toasted bread crumbs on the top."

"You should make it for me sometime."

Of course that would never happen. But the idea of it caused heat to rise from her neck, spreading up to her hairline. "Shelby wouldn't like it."

"No. She doesn't eat carbs."

"I meant me cooking for you."

Mark said nothing, only looked out the window with a distracted expression. Was he thinking of Shelby? Anticipating seeing her soon?

"What would you serve with it?" he asked after a moment.

Maggie's grin fractured into a laugh. "I'd serve it as a main course with grilled asparagus on the side . . . and maybe a tomato and arugula salad." It seemed like forever since she'd made anything beyond the simplest meals for herself, since cooking for one rarely seemed worth the effort. "I love to cook."

"We have something in common."

"You love to cook, too?"

"No, I love to eat."

"Who does the cooking at your house?"

"My brother Sam and I take turns. We're both terrible."

"I have to ask: How in the world did you end up deciding to raise Holly together?"

"I knew I couldn't do it alone. But there was no one else, and I couldn't put Holly into foster care. So I guilted Sam into helping."

"No regrets?"

Mark shook his head immediately. "Losing my sister was the worst thing that's ever happened to me, but having Holly in my life is the best. Sam would say the same."

"Has it been what you expected?"

"I didn't know what to expect. We take it day by day. There are great moments . . . the first time Holly caught a fish at Egg Lake . . . or one morning when she and Sam decided to build a waffle tower with bananas and marshmallows for breakfast . . . you should have seen the kitchen. But there are the other moments, when we're out somewhere and we see a family . . ." He hesitated. "And I see it in Holly's face, wondering what it would be like to have one."

"You *are* a family," Maggie said.

"Two uncles and a kid?"

"Yes, that's a family."

As they continued to talk, it somehow slipped into the bonelessly comfortable, unstructured conversation of longtime friends, both of them letting it go where it would.

She told him what it was like to have lived in a big family—the endless competition for hot water, for attention, for privacy. But even with the squabbling and rivalry, they had been affectionate and happy, and had taken care of each other. By the time Maggie was in fourth grade, she had known how to cook dinner for ten. She had worn nothing but hand-me-downs and never thought a thing about it. The only thing she had truly minded was that possessions were always lost or broken. "You get to a point where you can't let it matter," she said. "So even as a little girl I developed a Buddhist-like nonattachment to my toys. I'm good at letting go of things."

Although Mark was hardly verbose when it came to discussing his family, there were a few spare revelations. Maggie gathered that the Nolan parents had been absorbed in their private war of a marriage while their offspring sustained the collateral damage. Holidays, birthdays, family occasions—all set the stage for routine showdowns.

"We stopped having Christmas when I was fourteen," Mark told her.

Maggie's eyes widened. "Why?"

"It started because of a bracelet my mom saw while she was out with Victoria. It was in a store window, and they went in and she tried it on, and told Vick she had to have it. So they came home all excited, and from then on, all Mom talked about was how much she wanted that bracelet for Christmas. She gave Dad the information about it, and kept asking had he done anything about it, when was he going to get it, and it became this huge deal. So Christmas morning came, and there was no bracelet."

"What did he give her instead?" Maggie asked, fascinated and appalled.

"I don't remember. A blender or something. Anyway, Mom was so angry that she said we would never have a family Christmas again."

"Ever?"

"Ever. I think she'd been looking for an excuse, and that was it. And we were all relieved. From then on we all went our separate ways for Christmas, spent it at friends' houses, or went to a movie or something." Seeing her expression, he felt the need to add, "It was really fine. Christmas never meant what it was supposed to, for us. But here's the weird part of the story: Victoria felt so bad about the whole thing that she got Sam and Alex and me to pitch in and buy the bracelet for Mom's birthday. We all worked and saved up for it, and Victoria wrapped it in fancy paper with a big bow. And when Mom opened it, we were expecting some huge reaction—tears of joy, something like that. But instead . . . it was like she didn't remember the bracelet at all. She said, 'How nice,' and 'Thank you,' and that was it. And I never remember seeing her wear it."

"Because it was never about the bracelet."

"Yeah." He gave her an arrested look. "How did you know that?"

"Most of the time when couples argue, it's not really about the thing they're fighting about; there's a deeper reason why they're arguing."

"When I argue with someone, it's always about the thing I'm arguing about. I'm shallow that way."

"What do you and Shelby argue about?"

"We don't."

"You never argue about *anything?*"

"Is that bad?"

"No, no, not at all."

"You think it's bad."

"Well . . . I guess it depends on the reason. Is there no conflict because you happen to agree about absolutely everything? Or is it because neither of you is all that invested in the relationship?"

Mark pondered that. "I'm going to pick a fight with her as soon as I reach Seattle, and find out."

"Please don't," Maggie said, laughing.

It seemed they had only been talking for ten or fifteen minutes, but eventually it registered with Maggie that people were gathering their belongings, and preparing for the arrival at Anacortes. The ferry was crossing the Rosario Strait. A mournful blare irritated her into the

74

awareness that an hour and a half had disappeared with unbelievable speed. She felt herself coming out of something like a trance. And she reflected privately that the ferry ride to Anacortes had been more fun than anything she had done in months. Maybe years.

Standing, Mark looked down at her with a disarming half smile. "Hey . . ." The soft tone of his voice sent a pleasant prickling sensation along the back of her neck. "Are you taking the ferry back on Sunday afternoon?"

She stood as well, unbearably aware of him, her senses wanting to draw in the details of him: the heat of his skin beneath the cotton shirt . . . the place where the dark locks of his hair, shiny as ribbons, curled slightly against the tanned skin of his neck.

"Probably," she said in answer to his question.

"Will you be on the two forty-five ferry, or the four-thirty?"

"I don't know yet."

Mark nodded, letting it go.

As he left, Maggie was aware of a sense of unsettling pleasure, edged with yearning. She reminded herself that Mark Nolan was off-limits. And so was she. Not only did she distrust the intensity of her own attraction to him, but she wasn't ready for the kind of risk he presented.

She would never be ready for that.

Some risks you could only afford to take once.

Five

. . . .

Growing up in the Edgemoor neighborhood of Bellingham, Maggie and her brothers and sisters had explored the trails of Chuckanut Mountain and played along the shores of Bellingham Bay. The quiet neighborhood offered views of both the San Juans and the Canadian mountains. It was also situated next to Fairhaven, where you could browse through unique shops and galleries, or eat at restaurants where the waiters could always tell you about the freshest catch and where it had been brought from.

Bellingham lived up to its nickname of "the city of subdued excitement." It was laid-back, comfortable; the kind of place where you could be as eccentric as you wanted and you would always find company. Cars were bandaged with every kind of bumper sticker. Competing political yard signs sprang from people's lawns like spring-flowering bulbs. Any kind of belief was tolerated as long as you weren't pushy about it.

After Maggie's sister Jill picked her up in Anacortes, they went to the historic Fairhaven District for lunch. Since Maggie and Jill were the two youngest siblings in the Norris family, only a year and a half apart in age, they had always been close. They had gone through the school system one grade apart, attended the same camps, shared the same crushes on teen idols. Jill had been the maid of honor at Maggie's wedding, and she had asked Maggie to be the matron of honor at her upcoming wedding to a local firefighter, Danny Stroud.

"I'm glad we're stealing some private time," Jill said as they shared tapas at Flats, a small Spanish restaurant with oversized picture windows and a tiny outside patio lined with flower boxes. "Once I bring you to Mom and Dad's house, you're going to be swarmed and I won't get to talk to you at all. Except that tomorrow night, you're going to have to make a little time to meet someone."

Maggie paused in the act of lifting a glass of sangria to her lips. "Who?" she asked warily. "Why?"

"A friend of Danny's." Jill's tone was deliberately casual. "A very cute guy, very sweet—"

"Did you already ask him over?"

"No, I wanted to mention it to you first, but—"

"Good. I don't want to meet him."

"Why? Have you started going out with someone?"

"Jill, have you forgotten the reason I'm in Bellingham this weekend? It's the second anniversary of Eddie's death. The last thing I want to do is meet someone."

"I thought this would be the perfect time. It's been two years. I'll bet you haven't been on one date since Eddie died, have you?"

"I'm not ready yet."

Their conversation was interrupted as the waitress brought a bayona sandwich, a grilled pepper sausage and cheese on crusty peasant bread. It was always cut into three parts, the middle being the most succulent, smoky, and melting section of all.

"How will you know when you're ready?" Jill asked, after the waitress had left. "Do you have a timer that goes off or something?"

Maggie regarded her with exasperated affection, reaching for the bayona sandwich.

"I know a ton of cute single guys in Bellingham," Jill continued. "I could fix you up so easily. And there you are in Friday Harbor, hiding. You could at least have opened a bar or a sporting-goods shop, where you could meet men. But a toy shop?"

"I love my shop. I love Friday Harbor."

"But are you happy?"

"I am," Maggie said reflectively, after consuming a delicious bite of sandwich. "I'm really okay."

"Good, now it's time to go on with your life. You're only twenty-eight, and you should stay open to the possibility of finding someone."

"I don't want to have to go out there again. The chances of finding real love are about a billion to one. I had it once, and there's no way it will happen again."

"You know what you need? A provisional boyfriend."

"Provisional?"

"Yes, like when you get a provisional driver's license so you can brush up on your skills before you get the real one. Don't worry about finding a guy to have a serious relationship with . . . just pick someone fun to help you get on the road again."

"I guess that would make me a Class C dater," Maggie said, entertained. "Could I do that while unaccompanied by a parent or guardian?"

"Absolutely," Jill said, "as long as you practice safe driving."

After lunch, they stopped by Rocket Donuts at Maggie's insistence. She ordered a selection of doughnuts that included oblong confections covered with maple frosting and topped with strips of bacon, doughnuts crusted with chunks of Oreo cookies, and fried cake doughnuts drenched in Guittard Chocolate.

"Those are for Dad, of course," Jill said.

"Yep."

"Mom will kill you," Jill said. "She's been trying to cut back his cholesterol."

"I know. But he texted me this morning, begging me to bring him a box."

"You're an enabler, Maggie."

"I know. That's why he loves me best."

The long driveway leading up to the house was

congested with a half-dozen vehicles, the three-quarter-acre lot swarming with children. A few of them ran to Maggie, one of them showing her where he had lost a tooth, another trying to entice her into a game of hide-and-seek. Laughing, Maggie promised to play with them later.

Entering the house, Maggie went to the kitchen, where her mother and a group of siblings and in-laws were all busy cooking. She kissed her mother, a voluptuous but trim woman with a silver-gray bob and a beautiful complexion that had no need of makeup. She was wearing an apron that proclaimed: SEEN IT ALL, HEARD IT ALL, DONE IT ALL. JUST CAN'T REMEMBER IT ALL.

"Those are not for your father, are they?" her mother asked, with a stern glance at the box of doughnuts.

"It's full of celery and carrot sticks," Maggie said. "The box is just for presentation."

"Your dad's in the living room," her mother said. "We finally got surround sound, and he's been glued to the TV ever since. He says the gunshots sound real now."

"If that's what he wanted, you could have just driven him to Tacoma," one of her brothers said.

Maggie grinned as she went to the living room.

Her father occupied the corner of a big boxy sofa with a sleeping baby on his lap. As Maggie walked into the room, his gaze fell to the box of doughnuts in her arms. "My favorite daughter," he said.

"Hi, Dad." Leaning over, Maggie kissed him on the head and placed the box on his lap.

Her father rummaged through the box, found a maple-bacon doughnut, and began to devour it with an expression of bliss. "Come sit by me. And take the baby . . . I need two hands for this."

Carefully Maggie settled the warm, sleepy weight of the baby onto her shoulder. "Whose is he?" she asked. "I don't recognize this one."

"I have no idea. Someone handed him to me."

"Is he one of your grandchildren?"

"Could be."

Maggie answered questions about the store, and the latest goings-on at Friday Harbor, and whether she had met anyone interesting lately. She hesitated just long enough to make his eyes brighten with interest.

"Aha. Who is he, and what does he do?"

"Oh, it's no one, he's . . . there's nothing. He's taken. I talked to him on the ferry on the way over here." Feeling the baby twitch in his sleep, she put her hand on his tiny back, soothing him with a circling stroke. "I think I sort of accidentally flirted with him."

"Is that bad?"

"Maybe not, but it makes me wonder . . . how do I know when I'm ready to start going out again?"

"I'd say involuntary flirting is a sign."

"I feel weird about it. I was attracted to him even though he's nothing like Eddie."

Eddie, before his illness, had been sunny, lighthearted, a prankster. The man she had spent time with this morning was darker, quieter, with a reserve that hinted of deeply felt intensity. She hadn't been able to stop from imagining, in the most private corner of her mind, about physical intimacy with him, and it had seemed so potentially volatile that it had scared her. And yet that was part of the attraction. She remembered having wanted Eddie because he had been safe. But now she had caught herself wanting Mark Nolan for the exact opposite reason.

Lowering her head, Maggie kissed the sleeping baby in her arms. He was vulnerable but solid against her, his skin a miracle of smoothness and downy warmth. Briefly she remembered a moment in those last ephemeral days of Eddie's life when in quiet desperation, she had wished that she'd had a baby with him. Any way to keep a part of him with her.

"Sweetheart," her father said, "I've never had to go through what you did with Eddie. I don't know when the grieving process ends, or how you finally know when you're ready to move on. But there's something I'm sure of: The next guy will be different."

"I know. I knew that. I think what's bothering me is the realization that *I'm* different."

Her father gave her a vaguely owlish look, as if the comment had surprised him. "Of course you are. How could you not be?"

"Part of me doesn't want to change. Part of me wants to stay the same person I was when I was with Eddie." She stopped when she saw her father's expression. "Is that crazy? Do you think I need to see a therapist?"

"I think you need to go out on a date. Wear a nice dress, enjoy a free meal. Give someone a kiss good night."

"But once I move on from being Eddie's widow, who'll remember him? It'll be like losing him all over again."

"Honey." Her father's voice was quiet and kind. "You learned a lot from Eddie. The things about him that changed you for the better . . . that's how he'll go on. He won't be forgotten."

"I'm sorry," Shelby said, as Mark brought her a mug of hot tea. She was curled up on the sofa, dressed in gray cashmere loungewear. She was about to say something else, but instead let out a violent sneeze.

"It's fine," Mark said, sitting beside her.

Pulling a tissue from a box, Shelby blew her nose. "I hope it's just allergies. I hope you don't catch anything. You don't have to stay with me. Save yourself."

Mark smiled at her. "It takes more than a few

germs to scare me off." Opening a bottle of cold medicine, he shook out two tablets and handed them to her.

Shelby picked up a bottle of water from the coffee table, downed the tablets, and made a face. "We were going to such a great party," she said dolefully. "Janya has the coolest apartment in Seattle, and I was going to show you off to everyone."

"You can show me off later." Mark draped a throw blanket over her. "For now, focus on getting better. I'll even let you have the remote."

"You are so sweet." Sighing, Shelby leaned against him and blew her nose again. "So much for our sexy weekend."

"Our relationship is about more than sex."

"I'm glad to hear you say that." Pausing, she added, "That's number three on the list."

Mark flipped slowly through the cable channels. "What list?"

"I probably shouldn't tell you. But recently I read a list of five signs that a man is ready for the C-word."

Mark stopped channel-flipping. "The C-word?" he asked blankly.

"Commitment. And so far you've done three things on the list of what a man does when he's ready for commitment."

"Oh?" he said cautiously. "What's number one?"

"You've gotten tired of nightclubs and bars."

"Actually, I've never liked nightclubs."

"Second, you've introduced me to your family and friends. Third, you've just indicated that you think of me as more than an outlet for sex."

"What's four and five?"

"I can't tell you."

"Why not?"

"Because if I tell you, you may not do them."

Mark smiled and gave her the remote. "Well, let me know if I do. I'd hate to miss anything." He put his arm around her while she looked for a movie on demand.

The silences between them were usually comfortable. But this silence was tense, questioning. Mark was aware that Shelby had given him an opening. She wanted to set new parameters for their relationship, discuss where they might be headed.

Ironically, that was exactly what he'd wanted to bring up this weekend. There was every reason in the world for him to commit to Shelby, and tell her that he had serious intentions. Because he did.

If marriage with Shelby would be anything like dating her, it was what he wanted. No craziness, no screaming, no arguing. His expectations of the whole thing were reasonable. He didn't believe in fate or a great destined love. He wanted a nice, normal woman like Shelby, with whom there would be few surprises. They would have a partnership.

They would be a family. For Holly.

"Shelby," he said, and had to clear his throat, which had started to close up, before he could go on. "What do you think about . . . being exclusive?"

She turned in the crook of his arm to look at him. "You mean, you and me officially being a couple? Not seeing other people?"

"Yeah."

Shelby smiled in satisfaction. "You just did the fourth thing," she said, and snuggled back against him.

Six
. . . .

As anyone familiar with the Washington State Ferries system knew, ferry delays could happen at any time for a variety of reasons, including rough seas, low tides, onboard traffic accidents, medical emergencies, or maintenance issues. Unfortunately a "necessary repair to a vessel safety feature" was being given as the reason for a delay on the Sunday afternoon departure.

Having arrived an hour early to get a decent place in the long parking lanes leading to the ferry landing, Mark was left with time to kill and nothing to do. People were getting out of their cars, letting their dogs out, wandering to the terminal building to get refreshments or magazines. It was overcast and misty, an occasional cold raindrop breaking through.

Feeling restless and moody, Mark walked toward the terminal. He was starving. Shelby hadn't felt like going out for breakfast that morning, and all she'd had in the apartment was cereal.

It had been a good weekend with Shelby. They had stayed in and talked and watched movies, and on Saturday evening they had eaten Chinese takeout.

A breeze whipped directly from the Rosario Strait, bringing a clean salty scent, slipping into the collar of his light jacket like cold fingers. A shiver chased down his neck. He breathed deeply of the sea air, wanting to be home, wanting . . . something.

Entering the terminal, Mark headed toward the café, and saw a woman lugging a weekend bag to a nearby vending machine. A smile tugged at his lips as he saw her long streamers of red hair.

Maggie Conroy.

Thoughts of her had lurked in his mind all weekend. In idle moments, scenarios of how or when he might see her again had played in jaunty loops. His curiosity about her was relentless. What did she like for breakfast? Did she have a pet? Did she like to swim? When he had tried to ignore these questions, the fact of having something to ignore had made it all the more persistent.

He approached Maggie from the side, noticing the frown notched between mahogany brows as she studied the contents of the vending machine. Becoming aware of his presence, she looked up at him. The cheerful, quirky energy he remembered had been replaced by a vulnerability that went straight to his heart. He was caught off guard by the force of his response to her.

What had happened during the weekend? She'd been with her family. Had there been an argument? A problem?

"You don't want any of that stuff," he said, with a nod toward the array of glassed-in junk food.

"Why not?"

"Not one item in that vending machine has an expiration date."

Maggie scrutinized the display as if to verify his claim. "It's a myth that Twinkies last forever," she said. "They have a shelf life of twenty-five days."

"At my house they have a shelf life of about three minutes." He looked into her dark eyes. "Can I take you to lunch? We've got at least two hours, according to the ferry agent."

A long hesitation followed. "You want to eat here?" she asked.

Mark shook his head. "There's a restaurant down the road. A two-minute walk. We'll stow your bag in my car."

"There's nothing wrong with having lunch," Maggie said, as if she needed to reassure herself of something.

"I do it nearly every day." Mark reached for her overnight bag. "Let me carry that for you."

She followed him from the terminal building. "I meant, the two of us having lunch. Together. At the same table."

"If you want, we could sit at separate tables."

He heard a laugh stir in her throat. "We'll sit at the same table," she said decisively, "but no talking."

As they walked along the side of the road, the mist thickened into a drizzle, the air white and wet.

"It's like walking through a cloud," Maggie said, drawing in deep breaths. "When I was little, I used to think that clouds must have the most wonderful taste. One day I asked for a bowl of cloud for dessert. My mother put some whipped cream in a dish." She smiled. "And it was just as wonderful as I had imagined it would be."

"But did you know at the time that it was only whipped cream?" Mark asked, fascinated by the way the mist had provoked little wispy curls around her face.

"Oh, yes. That didn't matter, though . . . the idea of it was the point."

"I have problems trying to figure out where to draw the line for Holly," Mark said. "In the same classroom where she's learning that dinosaurs were real, they're also writing letters to Santa. What am I supposed to tell Holly about what's real and what's not?"

"Has she asked about Santa yet?"

"Yes."

"What did you tell her?"

"I said I hadn't decided one way or the other, but a lot of people believe in him, so it was okay if she wanted to."

"That was perfect," Maggie said. "Fantasy and make-believe are important for children. The ones who are allowed to use their imaginations are actually better at drawing the line between fantasy and reality than those who aren't."

"Who told you that? The fairy who lives in your wall?"

Maggie grinned. "Smart-ass," she said. "No, Clover wasn't the one who told me. I read a lot. I'm interested in anything having to do with children."

"I need to learn more." His voice turned quietly rueful. "I'm trying like hell to avoid ruining what's left of Holly's childhood."

"From what I can tell, you're doing fine." On impulse she caught at his hand, her fingers squeezing lightly in a gesture meant to reassure and offer comfort. Mark was pretty sure that was the way he was supposed to interpret it. Except that his hand closed over hers and turned the spontaneous clasp into something else. Something intimate. Possessive.

Maggie's grip loosened. Mark felt her indecisiveness as if it were his own, her unwilling pleasure in the way their hands fit together.

The press of skin to skin, such an ordinary thing. But it had set the axis of the entire earth off-kilter. He couldn't seem to assess how much of his reaction to her was physical and how much was . . . other. It was all tangled together in a way that was new and visceral.

Maggie tugged free.

But he still felt the imprint, the shape of her fingers, as if his pores had begun to absorb her.

Neither of them spoke as they went into the

restaurant, the interior fitted with polished dark wood, ancient scarred furniture, and wallpaper of indeterminate design. The air was scented with food, liquor, and slightly mildewed carpet. It was one of those restaurants that had undoubtedly been established with good intentions, but had gradually succumbed to the inevitability of a certain amount of tourist business, and had relaxed its standards. Still, it was a decent enough place to pass the time, and it offered a view of the strait.

An indifferent waitress came to take their drink orders. Although Mark usually drank beer, he ordered a whiskey. Maggie ordered a glass of house red, and then changed her mind. "No, wait," she said. "I'll have whiskey, too."

"Straight?" the waitress asked.

Maggie gave Mark a questioning glance.

"She'll have a whiskey sour," he said, and the waitress nodded and left. By this time Maggie's damp hair had renewed itself into buoyant zigzagging curls. He could easily become obsessed with them. Clearly any attempt to ignore his attraction to her was doomed. It seemed that everything he had ever liked in a woman, including things he hadn't even been aware of liking before, had been arranged in one perfect bouquet.

Before the waitress left, Mark had asked if he could borrow a pen, and she had given him a ballpoint.

Maggie watched, brows lifting slightly, as Mark wrote something on a paper napkin and handed it to her.

How was your weekend?

A smile crossed her face. "We don't really have to follow the no-talking rule," she told him. Setting the napkin down, she stared at him while her smile faded. A short sigh escaped her, as if she'd just finished a sprint. "The answer is, I don't know." Making a little face, she gestured with palms turned upward, as if to indicate that the issue was hopelessly complicated. "What about yours?"

"I don't know, either."

The waitress arrived with the drinks, and jotted down their lunch orders. After she left, Maggie took a sip of the whiskey sour.

"You like it?" Mark asked.

She nodded at once and licked the salty tang from her lower lip, a delicate flick of her tongue that made Mark's pulse jump in several places at once. "Tell me about your weekend," he said.

"Saturday was the second anniversary of my husband's death." Maggie's dark gaze met his over the rim of the glass. "I didn't want to be alone. I thought about visiting his parents, but . . . he was the only thing we had in common, so . . . I went to stay with my family. I was surrounded by about a thousand people all weekend, and I was lonely. Which makes no sense."

"No," Mark said quietly, "I understand."

"The second anniversary was different from the first. The first one . . ." Maggie shook her head and made a little gesture with her hands, a sort of sweeping-away motion. "The second one . . . it made me realize there are days when I forget to think about him. And that makes me feel guilty."

"What would he say about that?"

Hesitating, Maggie smiled into her whiskey sour. And for a moment Mark experienced an appalling stab of jealousy over the man who could still elicit a smile from Maggie. "Eddie would tell me not to feel guilty," she said. "He would try to make me laugh."

"What was he like?"

She drank again before answering. "He was an optimist. He could tell you the bright side of just about anything. Even cancer."

"I'm a pessimist," Mark said. "With occasional positive lapses."

Maggie's smile slid into a grin. "I like pessimists. They're always the ones who bring life jackets for the boat." She closed her eyes. "Oh. I'm getting a buzz already."

"That's okay. I'll make sure you get back to the ferry."

Her hand had crept across the table. She let the backs of her half-curled fingers touch his, a tentative gesture that Mark didn't know how to interpret. "I talked to my dad this weekend," she said. "He's never been the kind of parent who told me what to do; in fact, I probably could have done with a little more parental supervision while I was growing up. But he told me that I should go on a date with someone. A date. They don't even call it that anymore."

"What do they call it?"

"Going out, I guess. What do you say to Shelby when you want to spend the weekend with her?"

"I ask if I can spend the weekend with her." Mark turned his hand upward, opening his palm. "So are you going to take your dad's advice?"

She nodded reluctantly. "But I've always hated the whole process," she said feelingly, staring into her drink. "Meeting new people, the awkwardness, the despair of being stuck with someone for an entire evening when you know within the first five minutes that he's a dud. I wish it was like Chatroulette, and you could 'next' someone right away. The worst part is when you both run out of things to talk about." Without realizing it, Maggie had started to play with his hand, absently investigating the crooks of his fingers. He felt the pleasure of her touch all along his arm, responsive chords resonating along nerve pathways.

"I can't picture you running out of things to talk about," Mark said.

"Oh, it happens. Especially when the person I'm talking with is too nice. A good conversation always involves a certain amount of complaining.

I like to bond over mutual hatreds and petty grievances."

"What's your top petty grievance?"

"Calling customer service and never getting to talk to a person."

"I hate it when waiters try to memorize your order instead of writing it down. Because they hardly ever get everything right. And even if they do, it causes me a lot of stress until the food gets to the table."

"I hate it when people shout into their cell phones."

"I hate the phrase 'No pun intended.' It's pointless."

"I say that sometimes."

"Well, don't. It annoys the hell out of me."

Maggie grinned. Then, seeming to realize that she was toying with his hand, she flushed and pulled back. "Is Shelby nice?"

"Yes. But I tolerate it." Mark reached for his whiskey and finished it with an efficient swallow. "My theory about meeting people," he said, "is that it's better not to make a really good first impression. Because it's all downhill from there. You're always having to live up to that first impression, which was just an illusion."

"Yes, but if you don't make a great first impression, you may never get the chance to make a second one."

"I'm a single guy with a paycheck," he said. "I always get a second chance."

Maggie laughed.

The waitress brought their food and collected their empty glasses. "Another round?" she asked.

"I wish I could," Maggie said wistfully, "but I can't."

"Why not?" Mark asked.

"I'm barely sober." To demonstrate, she crossed her eyes.

"You only have to stop when you're not sober," Mark said, and nodded to the waitress. "Bring another round."

"Are you trying to get me drunk?" Maggie asked after the waitress had left, giving him a mock-suspicious glance.

"Yes. My plan is to get you drunk and then take you on a wild, crazy ferry ride." He pushed a glass of water in her direction. "Drink this before you start on your next one."

While Maggie sipped the water, Mark told her about his weekend with Shelby, and her list of things a man did when he was ready for commitment. "But she wouldn't tell me the fifth thing," he said. "What do you think it is?"

As Maggie considered the possibilities, her face went through a series of adorable contortions: a crinkling of the nose, a squint, a brief gnawing of her lower lip. "House-hunting?" she suggested. "Or talking about having children?"

"God." He grimaced at the thought. "I have Holly. That's enough for now."

"What about more later?"

"I don't know. I want to make sure I've done right by Holly before I even think about more kids."

Her gaze was sympathetic. "Your life has changed a lot, hasn't it?"

Mark searched for ways to describe it, feeling awkward in his desire to connect with her. He had never been given to confiding in others, had never seen the point in it. Receiving sympathy was one step removed from being pitied, which to him was a fate worse than death. But Maggie had a knack of asking questions in a way that made him want to answer.

"You look at everything differently," he said. "You start thinking about what kind of world you're going to send her out into. I worry about what kind of subliminal crap she's getting from TV, and if there's cadmium or lead in her toys. . . ." Mark paused. "Did you want kids with . . . him?" He found himself reluctant to say her husband's name, as if the syllables were invisible shims being tapped into place between them.

"Once I thought I did. Not now, though. I think that's one of the reasons I love my store so much— it's a way to be surrounded by children without having the responsibility."

"Maybe when you get married again."

"Oh, I'll never get married again."

Mark tilted his head in a silent question, watching her closely.

"I've done it once," Maggie said, "and I'll never

regret it, but . . . it was enough. Eddie fought the cancer for a year and a half, and it took everything I had to be there for him, to be strong. Now there's not enough left of me to give to anyone else. I can be with someone, but not belong with someone. Does that make sense?"

For the first time in Mark's adult life, he wanted to hold a woman for unselfish reasons. Not in passion, but to offer comfort. "It makes sense that you would feel that way," he said gently. "But that may not last forever."

They finished lunch and walked back to the ferry terminal, the rain so light and slow that you could practically see suspended droplets in the air. You could feel the sky pressing downward. The world was painted in shades of steel blue and pale gray, with Maggie's hair holding an intensity of red beyond red, every lock an inviting sine wave finished in a neat coil.

Mark would have given anything to play with those striated curls, to fill his hands with them. He was tempted to reach for her hand as they walked. But casual contact was no longer an option . . . because there was nothing casual about the way he wanted her.

Maybe his attraction to Maggie was simply a result of having just made a commitment to Shelby, and his subconscious was trying to find an escape route? . . . *Stay on course,* he told himself. *Don't get distracted.*

Their conversation was temporarily interrupted by the necessities of driving the car onto the ferry and finding seats on the main passenger deck. After that they occupied the same bench, talking about everything and nothing. Their occasional silences felt like the peaceful interludes after sex, when you lay there steeped in sweat and endorphins.

Mark was trying hard not to imagine sex with Maggie. Taking her to bed and doing everything to her, deep-pitched and half speed, improvised, and stretched out, and repeated. He wanted her under him, over him, wrapped around. Her body would be pale, adorned with a few constellations of freckles. He would chart them, trace their paths with his hands and lips, find every secret pattern and shiver and pulse—

The ferry docked. Mark waited on the main passenger deck longer than he should have, reluctant to part company with Maggie. He was one of the last people to go downstairs to the parking lanes and get in his car. The sky was sherbet-colored and streaked with cirrus. He felt, as always, the relief of returning to the island, where the air was easier to breathe, softer, and the brisk tension of the mainland ceased. The shoulders of the passengers waiting on the deck dropped en masse, as if they had all been rebooted simultaneously.

Mark had to return to his car soon, or it would block the entire lane from moving off the ferry, and he would face the justifiable wrath of dozens of drive-on passengers. But as he looked down at Maggie, every cell in his body resisted the idea of leaving her.

"Do you need me to drive you somewhere?" he asked.

An instant shake of her head, red waves swishing across her shoulders. "My car's parked nearby."

"Maggie," he said carefully, "maybe sometime—"

"No," she said, her smile gently regretful. "There's no room for friendship. No future in it."

She was right.

The only thing left was to say good-bye, something Mark was usually good at. This one was tricky, however. "See you around" or "Take care" were too indifferent, too casual. But any indication of how much the afternoon had meant to him wouldn't have been welcomed.

In the end, Maggie solved his dilemma by removing the need for good-bye. She smiled at his hesitation and set her hand to his chest, giving him a playful hint of a nudge.

"Go," she said.

And he did, without looking back, descending the narrow steel-lined staircase with echoing footsteps. He felt his heart beating strongly in the place her hand had touched. Getting into his car, he closed the door and fastened his seat belt. As he waited for a signal to pull forward, he had the tugging, nagging sense of having lost something important.

Seven

With the arrival of October, whale watching and kayaking were over for the year. Although tourists still came to San Juan Island, it was nothing compared to the deluge during the summer months. The question most often asked by tourists was how Friday Harbor had gotten its name. Maggie had quickly learned the two standard versions of the story. The one everyone preferred was the local lore that a sea captain, upon entering the harbor and seeing a man on shore, asked, "What bay is this?" The man, mistakenly hearing the question as "What day is this?" had replied, "Friday."

The truth, however, was that the harbor had been named after a Hawaiian, Joseph Friday, who had worked for the Hudson's Bay Company, tending sheep about six miles north of the harbor. When sailors came along the coast and saw the column of smoke rising from his camp, they knew they had reached Friday's bay, and the British had eventually charted it that way.

The island had transferred to American possession in 1872, and from then on industry had flourished. San Juan Island had been the fruit-growing capital of the Northwest. It had also been home to lumber and shake mills, and salmon-packing companies. Now the waterfront was crowded with upscale condominiums and pleasure craft instead of canneries and scows. Tourism had become the mainstay of the economy, and although it peaked during the summers, it was a year-round industry.

With autumn in the air, and the leaves in full color, the residents of San Juan Island began to prepare for the upcoming holidays. The island bustled with harvest festivals, farmer's markets, wine tastings, gallery events, and theater performances. Maggie's shop showed no signs of slowing down, as local customers came to buy Halloween costumes and accessories, and to take care of some early Christmas shopping. In fact, Maggie had just hired one of Elizabeth's daughters, Diane, as a part-time sales clerk.

"Now maybe you can ease up a little," Elizabeth told Maggie. "Taking a day off won't kill you, you know."

"I have fun at the shop."

"Go have fun away from the shop," Elizabeth said. "You need to have a conversation with someone who's over four feet tall." An idea occurred to her. "You should get a massage at that spa in Roche Harbor. They have a new masseuse named Theron. One of my friends says he has the hands of an angel." Her brows waggled significantly.

"If it's a man, I don't think it's a masseuse," Maggie said. "But at the moment I can't remember what you call a man who massages you."

"A weekly appointment is what I call him," Elizabeth said. "If he's single, you could ask him out."

"You can't ask a massage guy to go out with you," Maggie protested. "It's like a doctor-patient relationship."

"I dated my doctor," Elizabeth said.

"You did?"

"I went to his office and told him that I had decided to switch doctors. And he was very concerned and asked why. And I said, 'Because I want you to take me out to dinner on Friday night.'"

Maggie's eyes widened. "Did he?"

Elizabeth nodded. "We were married six months later."

Maggie smiled. "I love that story."

"We had forty-one years together, until he passed away."

"I'm so sorry," Maggie said.

"He was a lovely man. I wanted more years with him. But that doesn't mean I can't enjoy spending time with my friends. We travel together, e-mail each other . . . I couldn't do without them."

"I have wonderful friends," Maggie said. "But they're all married, and they were such a big part of my life with Eddie that sometimes . . ."

"The old memories get in the way," Elizabeth said perceptively.

"Exactly."

Elizabeth nodded. "You have a new life. Keep the old friends, but it doesn't hurt to add some new ones. Preferably single ones. Which reminds me . . . have the Scolaris introduced you to Sam Nolan yet?"

"How did you know about that?"

The older woman appeared vastly pleased with herself. "We live on an island, Maggie. Gossip has nowhere to go except in circles. So . . . have you met him?"

Maggie busied herself with rearranging some fresh lavender stalks in a vase shaped like a milk jug. The idea of going out with Mark's younger brother was intolerable. Every small resemblance —the shape of his eyes, or the pitch of his voice —would make the entire experience an exercise in misery.

And that would be unfair to Sam. Maggie would never be able to appreciate everything that he was, because she wouldn't be able to forget about everything that he wasn't.

Specifically, that he wasn't Mark.

"I told Brad and Ellen that I'm not interested in meeting anyone right now," she said.

"But Maggie," Elizabeth said, perturbed, "Sam Nolan is the most charming, good-natured young man in the world. And he's between girlfriends since he's been so busy with the vineyard. He's a winemaker. A romantic. You don't want to miss out on an opportunity like this."

Maggie gave her a skeptical smile. "Do you really think this young, charming single guy is going to want to go out with me?"

"Why wouldn't he?"

"I'm a widow. I have baggage."

"Who has no baggage?" Elizabeth clicked her tongue in chiding. "For heaven's sake, being a widow is nothing to feel awkward about. It means you're a woman with the spice of experience, a woman who has been loved. We know how to appreciate life, we appreciate humor, we enjoy our closet space. Believe me, Sam Nolan won't mind in the least that you're a widow."

Maggie smiled and shook her head. Picking up her bag from behind the counter, she said, "I'm going to walk over to the Market Chef and get some sandwiches for lunch. What do you want?"

"Pastrami melt with extra cheese. And extra onion." As Maggie reached the door, Elizabeth added cheerfully, "Extra everything!"

The Market Chef was an artisan deli that made the best sandwiches and salads on the island. There was always a crowd at lunchtime, but the wait was worth it. Looking into a glass case filled with fresh salads, pasta, perfect meat-loaf slices, and thick wedges of vegetable quiche, Maggie was tempted to order one of everything. She settled on Dungeness crab, artichokes, and melted cheese on toasted homemade bread, and ordered the pastrami melt for Elizabeth.

"For here or to go?" the girl behind the counter asked.

"To go, please." Seeing a stack of slablike chocolate-chip cookies in a glass jar near the register, Maggie added, "And under no circumstances should you add any of those."

The girl smiled. "One or two?"

"Just one."

"If you want to sit over there, I'll bring the sandwiches to you in just a minute."

Maggie sat by a window and people-watched as she waited.

In no time at all the girl approached with a white paper sack. "Here you go."

"Thank you."

"Oh, and . . ." The girl handed her a napkin. "Someone asked me to give this to you."

"Who?" Maggie asked blankly, but the girl had already hurried away to help a customer.

Maggie's gaze fell to the white paper napkin in her hand. Someone had written on it.

Hi

Looking up in bemusement, Maggie scanned the small seating area. Her breath caught as she saw Mark Nolan and Holly sitting at a bistro table in the corner. His gaze held hers, and a slow smile curved his lips.

The message on the napkin crumpled into Maggie's palm, her fingers tightening reflexively. A responsive ache of happiness awakened in her chest, just at the sight of him. *Damn it.* She had spent weeks trying to convince herself that the interlude she'd had with Mark had not been nearly as magical as it had seemed.

But that didn't explain the new habit of her heart to skip or stutter whenever she saw a dark-haired man in a crowd. It didn't explain why, more than once, she had awakened with the sheets tangled around her legs and her mind filled with the pleasant haze of having dreamed about him.

As Mark stood up from the table and walked to her with Holly in tow, Maggie was filled with a terrible, giddy rush of infatuation. Hectic color spread everywhere, right up to her hairline. Her heartbeat throbbed in every limb. She couldn't look directly at him, couldn't look fully away from him, just stood in unfocused confusion, bag in hand.

"Hi, Holly," she managed to say to the beaming child, whose hair was plaited in two perfect blond braids. "How are you?"

The child surprised her by darting forward and hugging her. Maggie automatically closed her free arm around the small, slender body.

Still hanging around Maggie's waist, Holly tilted her head back and smiled up at her. "I lost a tooth yesterday," she announced, and showed her the new gap in the bottom row.

"That's wonderful," Maggie exclaimed. "Now you have two places to put your straws when you drink lemonade."

"The tooth fairy gave me a dollar. And my friend Katie only got fifty cents for hers." This comparison was relayed with a hint of concern at the vagaries of such a pricing system.

"The tooth fairy," Maggie repeated, casting an amused glance at Mark. She knew how he felt about encouraging Holly to believe in fantasy creatures.

"It was a perfect tooth," Mark said. "Obviously a tooth like that deserved a dollar." His gaze swept over Maggie. "We were heading to your shop after lunch."

"Anything in particular you're looking for?"

"I need fairy wings," Holly told her. "For Halloween."

"You're going to be a fairy? I have wands, tiaras, and at least a half-dozen different pairs of wings. Would you like to walk to the shop with me?"

Holly nodded eagerly and reached for her hand.

"Let me carry that stuff for you," Mark said.

"Thank you." Maggie gave him the paper sack, and they left Market Chef together.

During the walk, Holly was talkative and lively, telling Maggie about her friends' Halloween costumes, and what kind of candy she hoped to get, and about the Harvest Festival she was going to after the trick-or-treating. Although Mark said little and walked behind them, Maggie was intensely aware of his presence.

As soon as they entered the shop, Maggie guided

Holly to a rack of fairy wings, all beribboned, glittered, and painted with swirls. "Here they are."

Elizabeth approached them. "Are we shopping for wings? How lovely."

Holly stared quizzically at the elderly woman, who wore a veiled cone hat and a long tulle skirt, and carried a magic wand. "Why are you dressed like that? It's not Halloween yet."

"It's my outfit for when we have birthday parties at the shop."

"Where?" Holly asked, casting an eager glance all around the shop.

"There's a party room in the back. Would you like to see it? It's all decorated."

After looking to Mark for permission, Holly went happily to the back with Elizabeth, skipping and hopping.

Mark looked after her with a wry, affectionate grin. "She bounces all the time," he said. His gaze returned to Maggie. "We won't stay long. I don't want to keep you from your lunch."

"Oh, that's no problem. How . . ." It felt like she had just taken a spoonful of honey, having to swallow repeatedly against the sweet thickness. "How are you?"

"Fine. You?"

"I'm doing great," Maggie said. "Are you and Shelby . . ." She had intended to say "engaged," but the word stuck in her throat.

Mark understood what she was trying to ask.

"Not yet." He hesitated. "I brought this for you." He set a tall, narrow-bodied thermos onto the counter, the kind that was capped by a drinking cup. Maggie hadn't noticed him carrying it before.

"Is that coffee?" she asked.

"Yes, one of my roasts."

The offering pleased her more than it should have. "You're a bad influence," she told him.

His voice was husky. "Hope so."

It was a delicious moment, standing there with him, imagining for one forbidden second what it would be like to take one step forward and erase the distance between them. To press up to him, against hardness and heat, and feel him gather her in.

Before Maggie could thank him, Elizabeth returned with Holly. The little girl, excited by the decorated party room and a big castle cake with candles on all the turrets, went immediately to Mark and demanded that he come see it, too. He smiled and let himself be towed away.

Eventually Mark and Holly piled up their purchases on the counter: a set of fairy wings, a tiara, and a green and purple tutu. Elizabeth rang them up, chatting amiably, while Maggie was busy helping a customer.

Maggie climbed a folding step stool to reach some figurines that had been stored in a cabinet above a display case. After retrieving Dorothy, the

Tin Woodman, the Lion, and Scarecrow, she told the customer that the Wicked Witch was out of stock. "I can reorder and have her here in about a week," Maggie said.

The customer hesitated. "Are you sure? I don't want to buy the others if I can't get the whole set."

"If you'd like, we'll call the distributor and make certain they can send the witch." Maggie glanced toward the cash register. "Elizabeth—"

"I have the number right here," Elizabeth said, brandishing a laminated list. She smiled as she recognized the customer. "Hello, Annette. Is this going to be a present for Kelly? I knew she would love that movie."

"She's watched it at least five times," the woman replied with a laugh, and went to the counter as Elizabeth dialed the phone.

Gathering up an armload of extra figurines, Maggie climbed the step stool and began to replace them in the cabinet. She began to struggle with her balance when some of the boxes shifted in her arms.

A pair of hands came to her waist, steadying her. Maggie froze briefly as she comprehended that Mark was standing behind her. The pressure of his touch was firm, capable, respectful. But the warmth of his hands sank through the thin cotton layer of her T-shirt, and it sent her pulse rocketing. She tensed against the compulsion to turn in the compass of his arms. How good it would feel to sink her fingers into that dark, heavy hair, and pull him closer, harder—

"Can I put those away for you?" he asked.

"No, I . . . I've got it."

His hands lowered, but he stayed nearby.

Maggie fumbled with the remaining boxes, pushing them blindly into the cabinet. Descending from the step stool, she turned to face Mark. They were standing too close. He smelled like sun, sea air, salt—the fragrance teased her senses. "Thank you," she managed to say. "And thanks for the coffee. How will I get the thermos back to you?"

"I'll come back for it later."

Having rung up the other customers, Elizabeth approached them. "Mark, I've been trying to convince Maggie to meet Sam. Don't you think they would have a good time together?"

Holly's face lit up at the suggestion. "You would like my uncle Sam a lot," she told Maggie. "He's funny. And he has a Blu-ray player."

"Well, those are my two requirements," Maggie replied with a grin. She glanced up at Mark, whose face had gone expressionless. "Would I like him?" she dared to ask.

"You don't have much in common."

"They're both young and single," Elizabeth protested. "What else do they have to have in common?"

Now Mark was wearing a distinct scowl. "You want to be introduced to Sam?" he asked Maggie.

She shrugged. "I'm pretty busy."

"Let me know when you decide. I'll take care of it." He gestured to Holly. "Time to go."

"Bye!" the little girl said brightly, coming forward to hug Maggie again.

"Bye, Holly."

After the pair had left, Maggie glanced around the shop, which had cleared out for the time being. "Let's have lunch," she told Elizabeth. They went to the room at the back of the shop and sat at the table, keeping their ears tuned for the telltale jingle of the bell on the door. While Elizabeth unwrapped the sandwiches, Maggie unscrewed the top of the thermos. An enticing scent wafted upward—toasty, rich, and cedary.

Maggie inhaled deeply, closing her eyes to concentrate on the heady fragrance.

"Now I understand," she heard Elizabeth say.

Maggie opened her eyes. "Understand what?"

"Why you weren't interested in meeting Sam."

A breath stuck in her throat. "Oh . . . I . . . it has nothing to do with Mark, if that's what you're thinking."

"I saw the way he looked at you."

"He's involved with another woman. Seriously involved."

"It's not over till the 'I dos' have been said. And Mark brought you coffee." This was stated as if the gesture was of incalculable significance. "It's probably the equivalent of Dom Pérignon."

Elizabeth cast a covetous glance at the thermos.

"Would you like to try some?" Maggie asked, amused.

"I'll go get my mug."

The brew was already creamed and sugared, a flow of light steaming caramel pouring into their cups. Silently they raised their coffees in a toast, and drank.

It wasn't just coffee . . . it was an experience. Smooth, roasted, buttery notes gave way to a velvet finish. Strength and sweetness, no trace of bitterness. It warmed Maggie down to her toes.

"Oh my," Elizabeth said. "This is delicious."

Maggie took another swallow. "It's such a problem," she said dolefully.

The older woman's face softened with understanding. "Being attracted to Mark Nolan?"

"He's off-limits. But whenever I see him, even though we're not flirting, it feels like we are."

"That's not a problem," Elizabeth said.

"It's not?"

"No, it's when it stops feeling like flirting that it becomes a problem. So go ahead and flirt—it may be the only thing that's keeping you from having sex with him."

Eight

· ·

On Halloween, Mark insisted that Sam be the one to take Holly to the activities in Friday Harbor, including a film show at the library, trick-or-treating at local stores, and a children's party at the fairgrounds. "Make sure to drop by the toy shop to see Maggie," Mark added.

"You sure?" Sam asked doubtfully.

"Yes. Everyone wants the two of you to meet, including Maggie herself. So go for it. Ask her out if you like her."

"I don't know," Sam said. "You have that look on your face."

"What look?"

"The look you get just before you kick someone's ass."

"I'm not going to kick anyone's ass," Mark said calmly. "She's not mine. I'm with Shelby."

"Then why does it feel like asking Maggie out would be rack jacking you?"

"It wouldn't be rack jacking. I'm with Shelby."

Sam had laughed quietly and scratched his head. "Your new mantra. Okay, I'll check her out."

Later Sam returned home with Holly, who'd had a wonderful time during the Halloween activies, and had filled an entire plastic pumpkin bucket with candy. Ceremoniously, they spread the candy on the table, surveyed it with admiration, and Holly chose two or three pieces to eat right then.

"Okay, upstairs to the bathtub," Mark had said, bending down to let Holly climb onto his back. "This is about the grimiest, stickiest little fairy I've ever seen."

"You don't believe in fairies," Holly said, giggling, as he carried her up the stairs piggyback.

"I do, too. I've got one right here."

After drawing her bath and putting a clean nightgown and towel on the closed lid of the toilet seat, Mark went downstairs. Sam had just finished putting the candy into a large Ziploc, and was straightening up the kitchen.

"So?" Mark asked gruffly. "Did you go into the shop?"

"About twenty of them. The town was crazy-busy."

"The *toy shop*," Mark said through gritted teeth.

"Oh, you're asking about Maggie." Sam reached into the fridge for a beer. "Yeah, she's a hottie. And Holly's crazy about her. She sat on the counter and helped Maggie hand out candy. I think she would've stayed there all night if I'd let her." He paused, tilting back the beer. "But I'm not going to ask Maggie out."

Mark watched him alertly. "Why not?"

"She gave me the Heisman."

"The what?"

"You know—" Sam mimicked the outstretched blocking arm of the Heisman Trophy pose. "She was friendly, but not interested."

"Well, she should be," Mark said in annoyance. "You're single, decent-looking . . . what's her problem?"

Sam shrugged. "She's a widow. Maybe she's not finished grieving for her husband."

"It's time for her to be finished," Mark said. "It's been two years. She needs to start living again. She needs to take a chance on someone."

"Like you?" Sam asked perceptively.

Mark shot him a dark glance. "I'm with Shelby."

"Yeah, I got that," Sam said with a quiet laugh. "Keep repeating it. Maybe at some point you'll start believing it."

Mark went upstairs, disgruntled. He told himself it wasn't his business if or when Maggie started going out again. Why, then, did the situation bother him so much?

He found Holly in her room, dressed in her pink nightgown, waiting in bed for him to tuck her in. The bedside lamp was on, warm light glowing through the pink lampshade. Holly's gaze was fixed on the pair of fairy wings, which were hanging on the back of a chair. Her fair ivory skin was dappled with red patches. Mark's heart was wrenched with concern when he saw that her eyes were wet.

Sitting on the edge of the mattress, he pulled her up against him. "What is it?" he whispered. "What's the matter?"

Holly's voice was muffled. "I wish my mom could have seen me in my costume."

Mark kissed her light hair and the delicate curve of her ear. And for a long time he just held her. "I miss her, too," he finally said. "I think she's watching over you, even though you can't see or hear her."

"Like an angel?"

"Yes."

"Do you believe in angels?"

"Yes," Mark said without hesitation, despite everything he had ever said or thought to the contrary. Because there was no reason for him not to allow for the possibility, especially if it comforted Holly.

Holly drew back to look at him. "I didn't think you would."

"I do," Mark said. "Faith is a choice. I can believe in angels if I want to."

"I believe in them, too."

Mark smoothed her hair. "No one's ever going to replace your mom. But I love you as much as she did, and I'll always take care of you. And so will Sam."

"And Uncle Alex."

"And Uncle Alex. But I was thinking . . . what if I marry someone who would help me to take care of you, and love you in a mom-type way? Would you like that?"

"Uh-huh."

"What about Shelby? You like her, right?"

Holly considered that. "Did you fall in love with her?"

"I care about her. A lot."

"You're not supposed to marry someone if you don't fall in love with her."

"Well, love is a choice, too."

Holly shook her head. "I think it's something that happens to you."

Mark smiled into her small, earnest face. "Maybe it's both," he said, and tucked her in.

The following weekend, Mark went to Seattle to visit Shelby. Her cousin's engagement party would be held on Friday night at the Seattle Yacht Club on Portage Bay. It was yet another step in the progression of their relationship: attending a family event, meeting Shelby's parents for the first time. He expected to get along well with them. From her descriptions, they seemed like decent, normal people.

"You will love them, I promise," Shelby had told him. "And they will love you."

The word "love" made Mark tense. So far, he and Shelby had not gotten to the point when either of them had said "I love you," but Mark sensed that she wanted to. And it made him feel as guilty as hell, because he wasn't looking forward to it. Of course he would say it back. And he would mean it, but probably not in the way that she wanted him to mean it.

A few months ago, Mark would have assumed that love was an ability he lacked. But Holly had disproved that entirely. Because the feeling of wanting to protect Holly, to give her everything, this soul-deep urge to make her happy . . . it was unquestionably love. Nothing Mark had ever felt before came close.

On Friday afternoon Mark took a flight to Seattle, worried as hell because Holly had come home from school with a slight fever. Ninety-nine point nine. "I should cancel," he had told Sam.

"You're kidding, right? Shelby would kill you. I got it covered. Holly will be fine."

"Don't let her stay up late," Mark had said sternly. "Don't let her eat crap. Don't miss her next dose of ibuprofen, or—"

"Yeah, I know. Everything's fine."

"If Holly's still sick tomorrow, the pediatrician's office is open until noon on Saturdays—"

"I know. I know all the stuff you know. If you don't leave now, you're gonna miss your flight."

Mark had left reluctantly after dosing Holly with ibuprofen. He had left her resting on the sofa, watching a movie. She looked small and fragile, her cheeks colorless. It bothered him to leave her, even though Sam had assured him everything would be all right. "I'll have my cell phone with me," he had told her. "If you want to talk to me, if you need me, you call whenever you want. Okay, sweetheart?"

"Okay." And Holly had given him the toothy little grin that never failed to melt his heart. Leaning over her, he kissed her forehead, and they rubbed noses.

It felt wrong to walk out of the house and go to the airport. Every instinct prompted him to stay. But Mark knew how much the weekend meant to Shelby, and he had no desire to hurt or embarrass her by not showing up to a family event.

In Seattle, Shelby picked him up at the airport in her sleek BMW Z4. She wore a sexy black dress and high-heeled pumps, her blond hair styled loose and straight. A beautiful, classy woman. *Any guy would be lucky to have her,* he thought. He liked Shelby. He admired her. He enjoyed her company. But the lack of turbulence and intensity between them, which had always seemed so right before, had begun to seem vaguely wrong.

"We're meeting Bill and Allison for dinner before the party," Shelby said. Allison had been her best friend since college, and was now the mother of three children.

"Great." Mark hoped he would be able to get his mind off Holly long enough to enjoy dinner. Pulling out his phone, he checked to see if there were any messages from Sam.

Nothing.

Noticing his frown, Shelby asked, "How's Holly? Still under the weather?"

Mark nodded. "She's never been sick before. At least, not since she's been with me. She had a fever when I left."

"She'll be fine," came Shelby's soothing reply. A smile curved her lightly glossed lips. "I think you're sweet to be so concerned about her."

They went to a casually sophisticated restaurant in downtown Seattle, the main room dominated by a twenty-foot central tower of wine bottles. They ordered an excellent pinot noir for the table, and Mark drained his glass quickly, hoping it would help him to relax.

It had begun to rain outside, water glittering on the windows. The rain was slow but steady, the clouds piled like unfolded laundry. Buildings crouched patiently beneath the elements, letting the storm water run through paved cascades and across vegetated swales, and into roadside rain gardens. Seattle was a city that knew what to do with water.

As Mark watched the oblique patterns of rivulets sliding along building exteriors of stone and glass, he couldn't help thinking of the rainy night, less than a year ago, that had changed everything. He realized that before Holly, he had measured out his emotions as if they were some finite substance. Now there was no hope of stopping or containing them. Was parenting ever going to get easier? Did you ever reach a point where you could stop worrying?

"This is a new side of you," Shelby said with a quizzical smile as she saw Mark checking his phone for the twentieth time during dinner. "Sweetie, if Sam hasn't called, that means everything's okay."

"It could mean something's wrong and he hasn't had a chance to call," Mark said.

Allison and Bill, the other couple, exchanged the smiling, slightly superior glances of experienced parents. "It's hardest with the first one," Allison said. "You're scared every time they get a fever . . . by the time you have the second or third, you stop worrying so much."

"Kids are pretty resilient," Bill added.

Knowing that all of this was intended to ease Mark's worry didn't help one bit.

"He'll be a good father someday," Shelby told Allison in a smiling aside.

The praise, which probably should have pleased Mark, elicited a flare of irritation. Someday? He was a father *now*. There was more to being a parent than a biological contribution . . . in fact, that was the least part of it.

"I need to leave for just a minute to call Sam," he told Shelby. "I just want to find out if the fever's gone."

"Okay, if it will help you to stop worrying,"

Shelby said. "Then we can enjoy the rest of the evening." She gave him a meaningful glance. "Right?"

"Right." Mark leaned over and kissed her cheek. "Excuse me." He stood from the table, went to the restaurant lobby, and pulled out his cell phone. He knew that Shelby and the other couple thought he was overreacting, but he didn't give a damn. He needed to know that Holly was okay.

The call was picked up. He heard his brother's voice. "Mark?"

"Yeah. How is she?"

A nerve-wracking pause followed. "Not great, actually."

Mark felt his blood turn to ice water. "What do you mean, 'Not great'?"

"She started throwing up not long after you left. She's been puking her guts out. I never would've believed one little body could produce so much evil stuff."

"What are you doing for her? Have you called the doctor?"

"Of course I did."

"What did he say?"

"That it's probably flu, and to give her sips of an oral rehydration fluid. And he said the ibuprofen may have made her sick to her stomach, so we're going to go with just Tylenol now."

"Does she still have a fever?"

"One hundred two, last time I checked.

Unfortunately she can't keep the medicine down long enough for it to do much good."

Mark gripped the phone tightly. He'd never wanted anything as much as he wanted to be back on the island, right then, taking care of Holly. "Do you have everything you need?"

"Actually, I have to pick up some stuff at the grocery store, like Jell-O and clear broth, so I'm going to get someone to babysit for a little while."

"I'm coming back."

"No, don't. I've got a whole list of people I can call. And I . . . oh, Jesus, she's throwing up again. Gotta go."

The connection went dead. Mark tried to think above the rush of panic. He called the airline for a reservation on the next flight to Friday Harbor, called for a cab, and strode back to the table.

"Thank goodness," Shelby exclaimed with a taut smile. "I wondered what was taking you so long."

"I'm sorry. But Holly's very sick. I have to go back."

"Tonight?" Shelby asked, frowning. *"Now?"*

Mark nodded and described the situation. Allison and Bill looked sympathetic, while Shelby appeared increasingly distressed. This sign of concern for Holly gave Mark a new sense of partnership with her, a feeling of connection. He wondered if she would consider going back with him. He wouldn't ask her to, but if she offered . . .

Standing from the table, Shelby touched his arm

gently. "Let's talk about this in private." She sent a somewhat weary smile in Allison's direction. "Back in a sec."

"Absolutely." And the two women exchanged one of those unfathomable female something-is-brewing glances.

Shelby went with Mark to the entrance of the restaurant, to a corner where they could talk undisturbed.

"Shelby—" Mark began.

"Listen," she interrupted gently, "I'm not trying to frame this as a choose-between-Holly-or-me thing . . . but she'll be fine without you. And I won't be. I want you to come to this party tonight, and meet my family. There's nothing you can do for Holly that Sam's not already doing."

By the time she had finished speaking, Mark's feelings of warmth and connection had vanished. No matter what she said, she was making him choose between her and Holly. "I know that," he said. "But I want to be the one doing it for her. And there's no way I could have a good time tonight, knowing my kid is sick. I'd be in a corner with my cell phone the whole time."

"But Holly's not yours. Not your own kid."

Mark looked at Shelby as if he'd never seen her before. What was the implication? That his concern for Holly wasn't valid because she wasn't his biological child? That he wasn't entitled to worry about her to this extent?

It was often in small moments that significant things were revealed. And with that spare handful of words, his and Shelby's relationship had undergone a sea change. Was he being unreasonable? Was he overreacting? He didn't give a damn. His first concern was for Holly.

When Shelby saw Mark's expression, she lifted her impatient gaze heavenward. "I didn't mean it to sound like that."

His brain methodically rearranged the words into a more precise truth. She had meant it, despite how it had sounded.

"It's okay." Mark paused, feeling the supportive trusses of their relationship being dismantled in this conversation, every word a hatchet-strike. "But she *is* mine, Shelby. My responsibility."

"Sam's, too."

He shook his head. "Sam is helping. But I'm her only legal guardian."

"So she needs *two* grown men hovering over her?"

Mark replied carefully. "I need to be there."

Shelby nodded and let out a slow breath. "Okay. Obviously there's no point debating this right now. Should I take you to the airport?"

"I called for a cab."

"I'd offer to come with you, but I want to be there for my cousin tonight."

"I understand." Mark put a hand on her back in a gesture of appeasement. Her spine was stiff and straight, as if it had been carved in ice. "I'm going to take care of dinner. I'll leave my credit card number with the hostess."

"Thank you. Bill and Allison will appreciate that." Shelby looked glum. "Call me later and let me know how Holly is. Although I already know she'll be fine."

"Okay." He leaned down to kiss her, and she turned her face so that his lips met her cheek.

Nine

The cab ride to the airport seemed to take forever. The flight back to Friday Harbor was so slow that Mark was certain he could have gotten there faster by kayak. By the time he'd driven back home to Rainshadow Vineyard, it was almost ten o'clock. An unfamiliar car was parked in the driveway, a white Sebring.

Mark entered the house through the back, walking straight into the kitchen. Sam was there, pouring himself a glass of wine. He looked haggard. The front of his T-shirt was water-splotched, and his hair was standing up in places. An array of medicine bottles and empty glasses had accumulated on the counter, as well as a plastic jug of rehydrating drink.

Sam looked at him with a flicker of surprise and shook his head. "I knew I shouldn't have told you," he said in resignation. "My God, Shelby must be pissed."

Setting down his bag, Mark stripped off his jacket. "I don't give a damn. How is Holly? Whose car is in the driveway?"

"It's Maggie's. And Holly's better. She hasn't thrown up for an hour and a half."

"Why did you call Maggie?" Mark asked, nonplussed.

"Holly likes her. And when I met her on Halloween, she told me to let her know if we ever needed help with Holly. I tried Alex first, but there was no answer, so I called Maggie. She came right over. God, she is great. While I was at the store, she put Holly in a lukewarm bath, cleaned things up, and got her to keep down some medicine."

"So the fever's gone?"

"For the time being. It keeps spiking, though. We'll have to keep checking on her."

"I'll take the night shift," Mark said. "You get some rest."

Sam gave him a weary smile and took another swallow of wine. "I could have handled it. But I'm glad you came back."

"I had to. I would have been rotten company at the party tonight, worrying about Holly."

"What did Shelby say?"

"She's not happy."

"She'll get over it. This is nothing that a bouquet of flowers and a little groveling won't fix."

Mark shook his head irritably. "I'm not above groveling. But it's not going to work out with Shelby."

Sam's eyes widened. "You're going to break up with her over this?"

"No, it's not this. It's just that lately I've realized . . . never mind, I'll tell you later. I have to see Holly."

"If the two of you split," Sam said as Mark headed for the stairs, "make sure that Shelby knows I'm available for revenge sex."

The hallway that led to Holly's room smelled like ammonia and bath soap. Lamplight sent a soft varnish across the rough wood flooring. For a moment Mark tried to imagine what an outsider's impression of the house would be: some of the unfinished rooms, the floors that needed sanding, the unpainted interiors. It was a work in progress. At this point, they had spent their efforts on structural restoration, making the house safe and sound, but they hadn't gotten around to doing much cosmetic work on it yet. No doubt Maggie had been appalled.

Entering Holly's room, he stopped just inside the doorway. Maggie was on the bed beside Holly, who was snuggled in the crook of her arm. A new stuffed animal was tucked on Holly's other side.

With her face bare of makeup, and her hair pulled back in a ponytail, Maggie looked like a teenager. There were scattershot golden freckles on her nose and the crests of her cheeks. She was reading aloud to Holly, who was glassy-eyed but peaceful.

Holly gazed toward Mark with drowsy confusion. "You came back."

Mark went to the bed and leaned over her, smoothing back her hair. His hand lingered on her forehead, testing her temperature. " 'Course I came back," he murmured. "I couldn't stay away if my girl is sick."

"I threw up," she told him solemnly.

"I know, sweetheart."

"And Maggie brought me a new teddy bear and gave me a bath—"

"Shhh . . . you're supposed to be falling asleep." He looked over at Maggie, and was caught by her dark gaze. He had to check himself from reaching out to touch her, from grazing his fingertips across the festive spray of flecks across her nose.

Maggie smiled at him. "One more page to finish the chapter?" she said, a question tipping her voice, and he nodded.

Drawing back, Mark sat on the side of the bed as Maggie continued to read. His gaze fell on Holly, her lids heavy, her breathing slow and steady. Tenderness and relief and anxiety tangled in his chest.

"Uncle Mark," the child whispered when the chapter was done. A small hand fumbled out to him across the quilt.

"Yes?"

"Sam said I could have"—she paused with a yawn—"a Popsicle for breakfast."

"That sounds fine." Mark lifted her hand and kissed it. "Go to sleep," he murmured. "I'll be watching over you tonight."

Holly settled deeper into the pillows and dropped off to sleep. Slowly, Maggie extricated herself, maneuvering off the bed. She was wearing jeans and sneakers, and a pink cotton sweater that had ridden up to her waist, revealing a strip of pale midriff. She flushed and pulled the hem of the sweater down, but not before Mark's gaze had flickered to an intimate flash of skin.

They left the room together, turning down the lamp but leaving a night-light glowing.

"Thank you," Mark said quietly, leading the way through the dim hallway to the stairs. "I'm sorry Sam had to call you. I should have been here."

"It was no problem. I had nothing else to do."

"It's no fun, taking care of someone else's sick kid."

"I'm used to sickness. Nothing bothers me. And Holly is such a sweetheart, I would do anything for her."

Mark reached for her hand and heard her breath catch. "Careful, the floor's uneven here. We haven't finished leveling it."

Her fingers folded, and so did his, their hands tightening into a compact and intimate sphere. She let him lead her to the stairs.

"The house isn't much to look at," Mark said.

"It's great. It has wonderful bones. When you're finished restoring it, it will be the most charming house on the island."

"We'll never be finished," Mark said, and she laughed.

"I saw two rooms that were beautifully

finished . . . Holly's room, and her bathroom. That says a lot." Slipping her hand free of his, Maggie took hold of the banister.

"Let me go first," Mark said.

"Why?"

"If you fall, I'll be able to catch you."

"I won't fall," she protested, but she let him precede her. As they went down the stairs, her voice descended on him like delicate petals. "I brought back your thermos. No thanks to you, I'm drinking coffee again. Although nothing tastes as good as the stuff you brought me."

"Secret ingredient."

"What is it?"

"I can't tell you."

"Why not?"

"If you could make it for yourself, you wouldn't come back for more."

A brief silence as she tried to interpret that. "I'm coming back tomorrow morning, to see Holly on my way to the shop. Does that mean I get a refill?"

"For you, unlimited refills." Reaching the bottom of the stairs, Mark turned and caught Maggie just as she began to stumble.

"Oh—" She gasped and reached out for him, her body colliding softly against his. Mark steadied her, settling his hands at her hips. A few of her curls brushed the side of his face, the touch of cool silk arousing him instantly. She was poised on the step, her weight still balanced on a forward pitch, entirely his to control. He was acutely aware of her, the warm, quick-breathing tension that he longed to soothe.

"The banister ends before the last step," he said. One of the house's innumerable quirks that he and Sam had adjusted to, but it always caught visitors unaware.

"Why didn't you warn me?" she whispered.

Her hands were on his shoulders. So easily, he could have urged her forward and kissed her. But he kept still, holding her in something that was almost an embrace. They were close enough that he could feel her breath stirring the air between them.

"Maybe I wanted to catch you," he said.

Maggie made a nervous sound of amusement, betraying how thoroughly she'd been caught off guard. He felt the subtle kneading pressure of her fingers, like a cat testing a new surface. But she gave no indication of what she wanted, made no movement toward or away, just stood in helpless waiting.

He moved back and guided her off the step, and led the way into the warm glow of the kitchen.

Sam had finished his wine and was pouring another. "Maggie," he said fondly, as if they had known each other for years. "My wingman."

She laughed. "Can a woman be a wingman?"

"Women are the *best* wingmen," Sam assured her. "Would you like a glass of wine?"

She shook her head. "Thanks, but I have to get back home. My dog needs to be let out."

"You have a dog?" Mark asked.

"I'm fostering him, actually. I have a friend who runs an animal rescue program on the island, and she talked me into taking care of him until she can find him a forever home."

"What breed is he?"

"A bulldog. He's got everything that can go wrong with a bulldog—bad joints, an underbite, skin allergies, wheezing . . . and to top it all off, Renfield has no tail. It was an inverted corkscrew and had to be amputated."

"Renfield? After Dracula's bug-eating hench-man?" Mark asked.

"Yes, I'm trying to make a virtue of his ugliness. In fact, I think there's something sort of noble about it. Renfield has no idea how hideous he is . . . he expects to be loved anyway. But some people can't even bring themselves to pet him." Her eyes sparkled, and a rueful grin crossed her face. "I'm getting desperate. I may end up being stuck with him."

Mark stared at her in fascination. She had a quality of uncalculated niceness that was as seductive as it was endearing. She wore the look of a woman who was meant to be happy, who loved generously, who would care for a dog that no one else wanted.

He remembered Maggie telling him that after

what she'd gone through with her husband's death, she had nothing left to give. But the truth was, she had too much to give.

Sam had gone forward to drape an arm around her shoulders. "You saved a life tonight," he told her.

"Holly's life was never in danger," Maggie said.

"I meant mine." Sam grinned at Mark. "You realize, of course, that one of us is going to have to marry her."

"Neither of you is my type," Maggie said, and a startled giggle escaped her as Sam dipped her, Valentino-style.

"You fill the empty void in my soul," Sam told her ardently.

"If you drop me," she said, "you're toast."

As Mark watched their clowning, he was suffused with jealousy. They were so at ease with each other, so comfortable—instant friends. And Sam's playful faux-wooing seemed a mockery of Mark's feelings toward Maggie.

"She needs to get home," he told his brother curtly.

Hearing the edge in his tone, Sam shot him an astute glance, and his smile widened. He brought Maggie upright, gave her a quick hug, and retrieved his wineglass. "My brother will walk you out to your car," he informed her. "I would offer, but I don't want to lose my drinking momentum."

"I can find my own way out," Maggie said.

Mark accompanied her anyway.

They went out into the November night, the

black-violet sky smudged by clouds, the air crisp and cold-bitten. Gravel gnawed at the soles of their shoes as they walked to Maggie's car.

"I have something to ask you," Mark said as they reached the vehicle.

"Yes?" she asked warily.

"What do you think about dropping the dog off with us tomorrow morning? He could spend the day with Holly. Maybe run a few errands with me. We'd take good care of him."

It was too dark to see Maggie's expression, but surprise laced through her voice. "Really? I'm sure Renfield would love it. But you wouldn't want to be seen with him." They stood beside the car, facing each other in the ghostly smudge of light that came from the kitchen windows. Mark's vision adjusted to the shadows. "Honestly, it's embarrassing taking Renfield anywhere," Maggie continued. "People stare. They ask if he had a run-in with a weed whacker."

Did she think he was intolerant? Narrow-minded? That his standards were so high that he couldn't handle, even for a day, the company of a creature who was less than perfectly attractive? Hell, had she gotten a good look at the house he lived in?

"Bring him," Mark said simply.

"Okay." A little puff of amusement, and then Maggie sobered. "You were supposed to spend the weekend with Shelby."

"Yes."

"Why didn't she come back with you?"

"She wanted to stay for her cousin's engagement party."

"Oh." Her voice lost its underpinnings. "I . . . I hope there's no problem."

"I wouldn't call it a problem. But it's not looking good for us right now."

An unfathomable silence passed. Then, "But you're so right for each other."

"I don't know that being right for each other is always the best foundation for a relationship."

"Being wrong for each other is?"

"Well, it gives you a lot to talk about."

Maggie chuckled. "All the same, I hope it works out for you." Turning to the car, she opened the door and tossed her handbag inside. She faced him again, her hair backlit from the interior lights of the dash.

"Thanks for taking care of Holly," Mark said quietly. "It means a lot to me. I hope you know that if you ever need anything, I'll be there for you. Anything at all."

Her expression was soft. "You're very sweet."

"I'm not sweet."

"Yes, you are." Impulsively she stepped forward to give him a hug, the way she had with Sam.

Mark's arms went around her. At last he knew the feeling of Maggie pressed all against him, breasts, hips, legs, her head against his chest, her weight balanced on her toes. They stayed together, compact and close, and began to let go at the same time.

But there was a shock of stillness, no longer than a heartbeat. And then in a motion that seemed as natural and inevitable as the inrush of a tide, they pulled together in another, even fuller embrace, securing more pressure, more heat. Every part of him strained for deeper contact. He pressed his face into her hair and filled his arms with her.

Her face was partially tucked against his neck, her breath a hot feathery caress on his skin, awakening dormant impulses, irresistible needs, unwelcome in their fierceness. Blindly he searched for the source of heat, the soft seam of her lips. He let himself kiss her, just once.

Maggie was shaking, urging herself against him as if seeking respite from the cold. Furtively he pressed his lips into the hollow behind her ear, drawing in her scent, her softness. Urgency made him clumsy at first, his parted lips dragging along the line of her neck, down to the collar of the pink sweater and back again. The thin skin of her throat lifted against his mouth as she gasped. Finding no resistance, he took her mouth in the full, deep kiss he craved. He searched her, tasted her, letting the sensation blaze into something raw and unrestrained.

Her response was hesitant at first, her mouth moving upward in a questioning stroke. Her body was light and pliant, molding tentatively against him. Feeling her balance faltering, he slid a hand low on her hips to bring her closer. His mouth found hers again. He kissed her until her throat was resonant with small pleasure-sounds and her fingers had climbed delicately into his hair.

But in the next moment she was pushing at him. The word "no" ghosted between them, so softly that he wasn't entirely certain she'd said it.

Mark released her at once, a sharp thrill of protest running through his body at the effort it took to let go.

Maggie staggered back a step, and leaned against her car, so clearly aghast that Mark might have found it amusing, had he not been violently aroused. He drew in deep passion-roughened breaths, willing his tortured body to calm down. And he forced himself not to reach for her again.

Maggie was the first to speak. "I shouldn't have . . . that wasn't . . ." Her voice faded, and she gave a despairing shake of her head. "Oh God."

Mark strove to sound normal. "You're coming back tomorrow morning?"

"I don't know. Yes. Maybe."

"Maggie—"

"No. Not now. I can't . . ." There was a strain in her voice, as if her throat had constricted against the threat of tears. She got into her car and started it.

As Mark stood on the graveled drive, Maggie maneuvered the car onto the main road and drove off without a backward glance.

Ten

The alarm clock awakened Maggie with indignant beeps, starting at a measured pace and then increasing in frequency and volume until it reached a series of voltaic shrieks that forced her out of bed. Groaning, stumbling, she reached the clock on the dresser and turned it off. She had deliberately set it far away from the bed, having learned in the past that when the alarm was on the nightstand, she was capable of repeatedly hitting the snooze button while still mostly asleep.

A scrabbling sound of claws on wood, and the bedroom door swung open to reveal Renfield's massive, square face with its pronounced underbite. *Ta-da!* his expression seemed to say, as if the sight of a half-hairless, wheezing, dentally challenged bulldog was the best possible way to start someone's day. The bald patches were a result of eczema, which antibiotics and a special diet had helped to calm down. But so far the fur hadn't grown back. Bad conformation had given him an awkward appearance when he walked or ran, a kind of diagonal lurch.

"Good morning, weirdo," Maggie said, bending down to pet him. "What a night." Fitful sleep, tossing and turning, vivid dreams.

And then she remembered why she'd gotten no rest.

A groan escaped her, and her hand stilled on Renfield's loose-skinned head.

The way Mark had kissed her . . . the way she had responded . . .

And there was no choice, she had to face him today. If she didn't, he might draw the wrong conclusions. The only option was to go to Rainshadow Vineyard and act like nothing had happened. She would be breezy and nonchalant.

Trudging into the bathroom of her one-bedroom bungalow, Maggie washed her face and blotted it with a towel. And she held the towel against her eyes when she felt the unexpected sting of tears. Just for a moment she let herself relive the kiss. It had been so long since she'd been held in passion, gripped hard and sure against a man's body. And Mark had been so strong, and so warm, that it was no wonder she'd given in to temptation. Any woman would have.

Some of the sensations had been familiar, but some had been entirely new. She could not remember ever having felt such pure hundred-proof lust, the astonishing heat shimmering all through her, and that seemed like a betrayal—and a source of danger. It was more than a little alarming to a woman who'd had enough upheaval for a lifetime. No wild, crazy, heart-wrenching affair for her . . . no more hurt, no more loss . . . what she needed was peace and quiet.

All moot points, however. Maggie had every reason to think that Mark would get back together with Shelby. Maggie had been a momentary diversion, a brief flirtation. There was no way that Mark would want to deal with the baggage Maggie carried; she herself didn't want to sort through it. Last night had meant nothing to him.

And she had to convince herself, somehow, that it had meant nothing to her.

Setting aside the towel, Maggie looked down at Renfield, who was panting and snorting beside her. "I'm a woman of the world," she told him. "I can handle this. We're going over there, and I'm dropping you off for the day. And you're going to try to be as nonweird as possible."

After dressing in a denim skirt, low-heeled boots, and a casual fitted jacket, Maggie applied a light touch of makeup. Pink blush, mascara, tinted lip balm, and concealer all helped to soften the ravages of a sleepless night. But was that too much? . . . Would it appear to Mark as if she was trying to attract him? She rolled her eyes and shook her head at her own absurdity.

Renfield, who loved to go places, was overjoyed when Maggie lifted him into the Sebring. He strained to push his head out of the car window, but Maggie kept a firm hold on his leash, fearing that her top-heavy companion might accidentally fall out of the vehicle.

The day was clear and cool, the sky pale blue with a thin froth of clouds. Feeling her nervousness increase the closer she got to the vineyard, Maggie took a deep restorative breath, and another, repeating the process until she was nearly as wheezy as Renfield.

The figures of Sam and his workers were out among the harvest vines, pruning the growth of the previous year, shaping the vineyard before they put it to bed for the winter. Pulling up to the house, Maggie stopped the car and looked at Renfield. "We're going to be casual and confident," she told him. "No big deal."

The bulldog pushed his head at her affectionately, demanding a petting. Maggie stroked him gently and sighed. "Here we go."

Keeping Renfield on his leash, Maggie took him to the front door, pausing patiently as he lumbered up each step. Before she could knock on the door, it opened, and Mark stood there in jeans and a flannel shirt. He was so sexy, his shirt rumpled, his dark hair disheveled, that Maggie felt a responsive pang deep in her stomach.

"Come in." His scruffy, early-morning voice was pleasant to her ears. She led the dog into the house.

A smile entered Mark's blue-green eyes. "Renfield," he said, and lowered to his haunches. The dog went to him eagerly. Mark petted him more vigorously than Maggie usually did, roughing up the rolls of his neck, rubbing and scratching. Renfield adored it. In the absence of a tail, he wagged his entire back end, managing something resembling a Shakira dance.

"You," Mark told the dog conversationally, "look like a Picasso painting. In his Cubist period."

Panting ecstatically, Renfield licked at his wrist and flattened slowly onto his stomach, his legs pointing in the four cardinal directions of the compass.

Even in her anxiety, Maggie had to laugh at the dog's slo-mo collapse. "Sure you won't change your mind?" she asked.

Mark glanced up at her with a lingering trace of amusement. "I'm sure." He unfastened the leash from the collar, stood to face Maggie, and gently took the handle from her. As their fingers brushed, she felt her pulse quicken to hummingbird speed, and her knees threatened to wobble. She thought briefly about how good it would feel to slide bonelessly to the floor as Renfield had.

"How is Holly?" she managed to ask.

"Great. Eating Jell-O and watching cartoons. The fever spiked one more time during the night, and then it was gone. She's a little weak." Mark studied her intently, as if he was trying to absorb every detail of her. "Maggie . . . I didn't mean to scare you last night."

Her heart began to pump hard and fast. "I wasn't scared. I have no idea why it happened. It must have been the wine."

"We didn't have wine. Sam had wine."

Heat shot to the surface of her skin. "Well, the point is, we got carried away. Probably because of the moonlight."

"It was dark."

"And it was late. Around midnight—"

"It was ten o'clock."

"—and you were feeling grateful because I'd helped with Holly, and—"

"I wasn't grateful. No, I *was* grateful, but that isn't why I kissed you."

Her voice was strung with desperation. "Basically, I don't feel that way about you."

Mark gave her a skeptical glance. "You kissed me back."

"As a friendly gesture. The way friends kiss." She scowled when she saw that he wasn't buying it. "I kissed you back out of politeness."

"Like an etiquette thing?"

"Yes."

Mark reached out and pulled her against him, his arms wrapping around her stiff body. Maggie was too stunned to move or make a sound. His head lowered, and his mouth was on hers in a firm, slow, devastating kiss that sent pleasure shuddering through her limbs. She went weak in a flush of heat, opening helplessly to him.

One of his hands wove gently into her hair, toying with the curls, shaping to her head. The world fell away, and all she knew was pleasure and need and a sweet, subversive ache that went all through her. By the time his mouth broke from hers, she was trembling from head to toe.

Mark looked directly into her dazed eyes, his brows lifting infinitesimally, as if to ask, *Point made?*

Her chin dipped in a tiny nod.

Carefully Mark eased Maggie's head to his shoulder and waited until her legs regained enough strength to support her.

"I've got to take care of some things," she heard him say over her head, "and that includes resolving my situation with Shelby."

Drawing back, Maggie looked up at him anxiously. "Please don't break up with her because of me."

"It has nothing to do with you." Mark brushed his lips over the tip of her nose. "It's because Shelby deserves a hell of a lot more than to be the woman someone settles for. I thought at one time that she would be right for Holly, and that would be enough. But lately I've realized it won't be right for Holly if it's not right for me, too."

"You're too much for me to handle right now," she said baldly. "I'm not ready."

His fingers played in her hair, combing slowly through the curls. "When do you think you'll be ready?"

"I don't know. I need a transitional person first."

"I'll be your transitional guy."

Even now, in her distress, he could almost make her smile. "Then who's going to be the guy after that?"

"I'll be that guy, too."

A despairing laugh escaped her. "Mark. I don't—"

"Wait," he said gently. "It's too soon for us to have this talk. For now, there's nothing you need to worry about. Come inside with me, and we'll go see Holly."

Renfield lumbered up and padded after them.

Holly was in the parlor off the kitchen, snuggled on the sofa in a cocoon of quilt and pillows. She had lost the glazed, fever-fretted look of the previous day, but she was still wan and fragile. At the sight of Maggie, she smiled and held out her arms.

Maggie went to the child and pulled her close. "Guess who I brought?" she asked against the light tangled banners of Holly's hair.

"Renfield!" the girl exclaimed.

Recognizing his name, the bulldog readily approached the sofa with his bulging eyes and perpetual grimace. Holly regarded him doubtfully, shrinking back as he put his front paws on the edge of the sofa and stood on his hind legs. "He's funny-looking," she whispered to Maggie.

"Yes, but he doesn't know it. He thinks he's gorgeous."

Holly chuckled, and leaned forward to pet him tentatively.

Sighing, Renfield rested his huge head against her and closed his eyes in contentment.

"He *loves* attention," Maggie told Holly, who began to croon and baby-talk to the adoring bulldog. Maggie grinned and kissed Holly's head. "I have to go now. Thanks for babysitting him today, Holly. When I come back to pick him up later, I'll bring you a surprise from the toy shop."

Mark watched from the doorway, his gaze warm and thoughtful. "Want some breakfast?" he asked. "We've got eggs and toast."

"Thanks, but I already had cereal."

"Have some Jell-O," Holly exclaimed. "Uncle Mark made three colors. He gave me some and said it was a bowl of rainbow."

"Really?" Maggie gave Mark a wondering smile. "It's nice to hear that your uncle uses his imagination."

"You have no idea," Mark said. He walked Maggie to the front door and gave her the tall thermos filled with coffee. Maggie was troubled by the cozy domestic feeling that had swept over her. The dog, the child, the man in a flannel shirt, even the house, a Victorian fixer-upper . . . it was all perfect.

"It doesn't seem like a fair trade," she said. "Special coffee, for a day with Renfield."

"If it means I get to see you twice in one day," Mark replied, "I'll take that deal any time."

Eleven

In the two weeks that followed, Maggie found herself seeing more and more of Mark Nolan. To her relief, it seemed that he had accepted that she was only interested in friendship. He frequently dropped by the toy shop with the thermos of coffee, and he also brought treats from a local bakery: crisp chocolate croissants, apricot pinwheels, sugared pastry sticks in white paper sacks. Now and then he coaxed Maggie to have lunch with him, once at Market Chef, and another time at a wine bar, where they lingered until Maggie realized that nearly two hours had gone by.

She was never able to turn down his invitations because she couldn't point to one instance in which Mark had put a move on her. In fact, he had done everything possible to allay Maggie's worries. There were no kisses or suggestive comments, nothing that indicated that he was interested in anything beyond friendship.

Mark had gone to Seattle to break up with Shelby, who had apparently taken it as well as could have been expected. When he told Maggie about it afterward, he didn't go into detail, but his relief was obvious. "No tears, screaming, or drama," he said. After a perfectly timed pause, he added, "Not from Shelby, either."

"You're still in the backslide window," Maggie said. "There's still a chance you may get back together with her."

"There's no backslide window."

"You never know. Have you already deleted her number from your phone?"

"Yeah."

"Have you returned all the things she left at your house?"

"She never got the chance to leave anything. Sam and I have a rule: no sleepover guests while Holly's in the house."

"So when Shelby visited you on the island, where did you and she . . ."

"We stayed at a bed-and-breakfast."

"Well," she said, "I guess it really is over. Are you sure you're not in denial? It's normal to feel sad when you've lost something."

"Nothing was lost. I've never thought of a failed relationship as a waste of time. You always learn something."

"What did you learn from Shelby?" Maggie asked, fascinated.

Mark pondered the question carefully. "For a while I thought it was good that we never argued. Now I realize it meant we weren't really connecting."

Holly soon asked for another day with Renfield, and Maggie brought him to Rainshadow Vineyard again. As they approached the house, Maggie saw that a small removable ramp had been set over part of the front steps. The top-heavy dog padded up the ramp, finding it much easier than trying to navigate the tall, narrow steps. "Is that for Renfield's benefit?" Maggie asked as Mark opened the door.

"The ramp? Yes. Did it work?"

"Perfectly." She smiled appreciatively, realizing that Mark had noticed the dog's previous difficulty with the steps, and had come up with a way to make it easier for him to go in and out of the house.

"You still trying to find a home for him?" Mark asked, holding the door as they entered the house. He bent to pet and scratch Renfield, who looked up at him with the grin of a medieval gargoyle, tongue dangling.

"Yes, but we're not having much luck," Maggie said. "He's got too many problems. He's probably going to need a hip replacement at some point, and there's his underbite, and his eczema. It's one thing to be high maintenance and cute, but high maintenance and looking like Renfield . . . no takers."

"Actually, if it's okay with you," Mark said slowly, "we'd like to keep him."

Maggie was stunned. "You mean on a permanent basis?"

"Yes. Why do you look so surprised?"

"He's not your type of dog."

"What's my type of dog?"

"Well, a normal one. A Lab or a springer. One that could keep up with you when you go for a run."

"I'll put Renfield on wheels. Sam and Holly spent the previous afternoon teaching him how to skateboard."

"He can't go fishing with you—bulldogs can't swim."

"He can wear a life jacket." Mark gave her a quizzical smile. "Why does it bother you that I want him?"

Renfield looked from Mark to Maggie and back again.

"It doesn't bother me . . . I just don't understand why you want him."

"He's good company. He's quiet. Sam says he's going to be great at keeping pests out of the vineyard. And most of all, Holly loves him."

"He needs so much care. He's got skin conditions. He needs a special diet, and special grooming products, and you're going to have a lot of vet bills. I'm not sure you understand everything that's ahead of you."

"Whatever it is, I'll deal with it."

Maggie didn't understand herself, the great swell of emotion that rolled through her. She lowered to her haunches and began to pet the dog, keeping her face averted. "Renfield, it looks like you've got a home now," she said, her voice husky.

Mark knelt beside her and cupped his hand under her chin, and urged her to look at him. His blue-green eyes were warm and searching. "Hey," he said softly. "What is it? Second thoughts about giving him away?"

"*No.* You've just surprised me, that's all."

"You didn't think I could make a commitment even when there are obvious problems ahead?" His thumb stroked over her cheek. "I'm learning to take life as it comes. Having a dog like Renfield is going to be inconvenient, messy, and expensive. But most likely worth it. You were right—there is something noble about him. Ugly on the outside, but damned if he isn't full of self-esteem. He's a good dog."

Maggie wanted to smile, but her chin quivered, and the flood of emotion was nearly overwhelming her again. "You're a good man," she managed to say. "I hope someday you'll find someone who appreciates you."

"I hope so, too." The words were edged with a smile. "Can we get up off the floor now?"

When Mark asked what Maggie's plans for Thanksgiving were, she told him that she had dinner with her parents in Bellingham every year. With the exception of the turkey, which her mother made, the rest of the meal was a huge potluck, with everyone contributing their best side dishes and pies.

"If you want to stay on the island this year," Mark said, "you could spend Thanksgiving with us."

Maggie experienced that feeling when she caught herself reaching for something that she had already decided not to allow herself: the last cookie on the plate, the one glass of wine too many. Spending a holiday with Mark and Holly was too much involvement, too much closeness. "Thank you, but I'd better stick to tradition," she said, forcing a quick smile. "My family's counting on me to bring mac and cheese."

"*The* mac and cheese?" Mark sounded forlorn. "Your grandmother's recipe with the four kinds of cheese and the bread crumbs?"

"You remember all that?"

"How could I forget?" He gave her a yearning glance. "Are you bringing back any leftovers?"

Maggie began to laugh. "You are shameless. I'll make an extra ramekin of mac and cheese for you. Would you like me to make a pie for you, too?"

"Would you?"

"What kind? Pumpkin . . . apple . . . pecan?"

"Surprise me," he said, and stole a kiss from her, so fast that she had no time to react.

The day before Thanksgiving, Maggie picked up Holly from the house at Rainshadow Vineyard, and brought her to her bungalow.

"Am I invited, too?" Sam had asked before they left.

"No, it's just for girls," Holly had told him, giggling.

"What if I wear a wig? What if I talk in a really high voice?"

"Uncle Sam," the child said cheerfully, "you're the worst girl ever!"

"And you're the best," Sam said, kissing her noisily. "All right, you can go without me. But you'd better bring me back a big pie."

Taking Holly to her house, Maggie put on some music, lit a fire in the fireplace, and tied one of her aprons around Holly. She showed Holly how to use an old-fashioned bell-shaped cheese grater, the kind with four sides. Although Maggie was going to use a food processor for most of the cheese, she wanted Holly to have the experience of grating some of it by hand. It was touching to see the child's delight in kitchen tasks of measuring, stirring, tasting.

"Here are the different cheeses we're going to use," Maggie said. "Irish Cheddar, Parmesan, smoked Gouda, and Gruyère. After we grate all of this, we're going to melt it with butter and hot milk. . . ."

The air was filled with good smells, with heat and sweetness, and a whiff of flour dust. Having a child in the kitchen reminded Maggie what a miracle it was that a few basic ingredients could be combined and heated into something wonderful. They made enough mac and cheese to feed an army, and topped it with bread crumbs that had been lightly browned in a pan with butter. They made two pies—one with satiny pumpkin filling, one with plump pecans—and Maggie showed Holly how to crimp a pie crust. They cut the extra scraps of dough into shapes, sprinkled them with sugar and cinnamon, and baked them on cookie sheets.

"My mother calls those scrap cookies," Maggie said.

Holly looked through the oven window at the pie-dough shapes. "Is your mother still alive?" she asked.

"Yes." Maggie set aside the flour-coated rolling pin and went to Holly. Kneeling behind her, she put her arms around the child, and together they looked into the oven. "What kind of pies did your mother make?" she asked.

"I don't think she made pies," Holly said reflectively, "but she made cookies."

"Chocolate chip?"

"Mmm-hmm. And snickerdoodles . . ."

It helped, Maggie knew, to be able to talk about those who were gone. It was good to remember. And they continued to talk as they baked, not in a long protracted conversation, but in little here-and-there sprinkles, the spice of memories mingling with the fragrance of warm pie crust.

When Maggie dropped Holly off in the evening, the child put her arms around her waist and held on for an extra-long hug.

Holly's voice was muffled against Maggie's front. "Are you *sure* you won't have Thanksgiving with us tomorrow?"

Maggie's tormented gaze went to Mark, who was standing nearby.

"She can't, Holls," he said gently. "Maggie's family needs her to be there with them tomorrow."

Except that she could, and they didn't.

Guilt and worry began to crowd out the good feelings that had blossomed during the afternoon. As she looked from the top of Holly's head to meet Mark's vaguely sympathetic gaze, Maggie comprehended how easy it would be to fall in love with both of them. And how much she would have to lose then, more than she could ever survive. But if she could somehow keep from getting seriously involved, she wouldn't have to risk having her heart broken beyond all hope of repair.

She patted Holly's back and gently disentangled herself from the child's enthusiastic grip. "I really have to go to Bellingham tomorrow," she said briskly. "Bye, Holly. It was a fun day." She bent and kissed the soft cheek, slightly flavored with cinnamon sugar.

On Thanksgiving morning, Maggie flat-ironed her hair, dressed in trouser jeans, booties, and a spice-colored sweater, and took the large foil-covered casserole dish out to her car.

Just as she began to back out of her driveway, her

cell phone rang. Stopping the car, she fished around in her bag until she found the phone amid the clutter of receipts, lip-gloss tubes, and spare change.

"Hello?"

"Maggie?"

"Holly," she said in instant concern. "How are you?"

"Great," came the little girl's cheerful reply. "Happy Thanksgiving!"

Maggie smiled, relaxing slightly. "Happy Thanksgiving. What are you up to?"

"I let Renfield outside to go to the bathroom, and then he came back in, and I put food in his bowl and gave him some water."

"I can tell you're taking good care of him."

"But then Uncle Mark made both of us leave the kitchen while they cleared out the smoke."

"Smoke?" Maggie's smile faded. "Why was there smoke?"

"Uncle Sam was cooking. And then they called Uncle Alex and he's taking the oven door off."

Maggie frowned. Why in the world would Alex be removing the oven door? "Holly . . . where is Uncle Mark?"

"He's looking for his safety goggles."

"Why does he need safety goggles?"

"Because he's helping Uncle Sam cook the turkey."

"I see." Maggie looked down at her watch. If she

was fast, she had enough time to drop by Rainshadow Vineyard and still make the late-morning ferry to Anacortes. "Holly, I think I'm going to stop by your house before I go to the ferry terminal."

"Great!" came the enthusiastic reply. "Except . . . maybe you shouldn't say that I called you. Because that might get me in trouble."

"I won't mention that part," Maggie assured her.

Before Holly could reply, a male voice in the background asked, "Holly, who are you talking to?"

Maggie said, "Tell him it's an opinion poll."

"A lady is doing an opinion poll," she heard Holly say.

A brief muffled consultation, then Holly said importantly, "My uncle says we don't have any opinions." A pause, and a few more muffled words. *"And,"* Holly added severely, "we're on the do-not-call list."

Maggie grinned. "Well, I'll just come over, then."

"Okay. Bye!"

It was cold and a little blustery, the perfect weather for Thanksgiving because it brought to mind images of cozy fireplaces, a turkey in the oven, and watching the Macy's parade on TV.

There was a BMW in the driveway, immaculate and sleek. The vehicle undoubtedly belonged to Alex, the Nolan brother she hadn't met. Feeling a little like an intruder, but driven by concern, Maggie parked and went up the front steps.

Holly met her at the door, dressed in corduroy pants and a long-sleeved tee featuring a cartoon turkey. "Maggie!" the girl cried, bouncing up and down, and they hugged. Renfield came up to them, panting and wheezing happily.

"Where are your uncles?" Maggie asked.

"Uncle Alex is in the kitchen. Renfield and I are helping him. I don't know where anybody else is."

A distinct odor of scorched food tainted the air, becoming stronger as they went to the kitchen. A dark-haired man was in the middle of disassembling the front of the oven, a power drill in his hand and a ponderous tool box beside him.

Alex Nolan was a smoother, more polished version of his older brothers. His features were handsome but remote, his eyes the crystalline blue of glacier ice. Like Sam, his form was lean and elegant, not quite so broad in build as Mark's. And his polo shirt and khakis, while casual, had the look of expensive garments.

"Hello," he said. "Who is this, Holly?"

"This is Maggie."

"Please, don't get up," Maggie said hastily, as he set aside the drill and made to stand. "Obviously you're in the middle of . . . something. Can I ask what happened?"

"Sam put some food in the oven and accidentally pushed the self-cleaning cycle button instead of the bake button. The oven incinerated the food and automatically locked, so they couldn't open the door and get the stuff out."

"Usually an oven unlocks when the temperature lowers to five or six hundred degrees."

Alex shook his head. "It's cooled down, and the door still won't open. It's a new oven, and this is the first time the self-cleaning cycle's ever been used. Apparently the locking mechanism is screwed up somehow, so I have to disassemble it."

Before Maggie could ask another question, she was startled by a flare of light, then an explosive rush of flame beyond the back door accompanied by a billow of smoke. Instinctively Maggie turned to shield Holly, and ducked her head with a gasp. "My God. What was that?"

Alex was staring at the back door, his face expressionless. "My guess is, that was the turkey."

Twelve

The back door flung open, and a large figure entered in a cloud of smoke. It was Mark, wearing safety goggles, his arms sheathed in massive gloves that extended up to his elbows. He strode to the sink, reached into the cabinet, and grabbed a fire extinguisher.

"What happened?" Alex asked.

"Turkey exploded when we lowered it into the fryer."

"Didn't you thaw it out first?"

"We've had it thawing in the fridge for *two days,*" Mark replied, with vicious emphasis on the last words. Noticing Maggie, he stopped short. "What are you doing here?"

"Never mind that, is Sam okay?"

"For now. But he won't be when I get my hands on him."

Another blinding flare came from outside, accompanied by fluent masculine cursing.

"Go put out the turkey," Alex suggested.

Mark gave him a dark glance. "Are you referring to Sam or the poultry?" He disappeared immediately, closing the door behind him.

Maggie was the first to speak. "Any method of cooking that involves getting dressed like a hazmat team . . ."

"I know." Alex rubbed his eyes. He looked like a man who hadn't slept well in a long time.

Glancing at the wall clock, Maggie realized that if she left right then, she would barely make it to the ferry on time.

She thought about Thanksgiving in her parents' home, the swarms of children, the crowded kitchen, her siblings and in-laws all busy peeling and chopping and mixing. And then the long, sociable meal . . . and that all-too-familiar feeling of being lonely in a crowd. Maggie wasn't needed there. Here, however, it was clear that she could be of some use. She looked down at Holly, who was leaning against her, and she patted her small back reassuringly.

"Alex," she asked. "Is the oven going to be operational at some point today?"

"Give me a half hour," he said.

Maggie went to the refrigerator, opened the door, and saw that it was fully stocked with eggs, milk, butter, and fresh vegetables. The pantry was equally well provisioned. With the exception of the turkey, they appeared to have everything that was necessary for a Thanksgiving dinner. They just didn't know what to do with it.

"Holly, honey," she said, "go find your jacket. You're coming with me."

"Where are we going?"

"We're going to run a couple of errands."

As the child scampered away to get a jacket,

Maggie told Alex, "I'll bring her back soon."

"I might not be here," he said. "As soon as I fix this, I'm going back home."

"To have Thanksgiving with your wife?"

"No, my wife's in San Diego with her family. We're divorcing. My plan is to spend the day drinking until I feel nearly as happy as I was when I was single."

"I'm sorry," Maggie said sincerely.

Alex shrugged, his voice cool. "Marriage is a crapshoot. I knew at the beginning that it had a fifty-fifty chance of working out."

Maggie regarded him thoughtfully. "I don't think you should get married unless you think it has a hundred percent chance."

"That's not realistic."

"No," Maggie admitted with a faint smile. "But it's a nice way to start." She turned to Holly, who had returned with her jacket.

"Before you leave, could you do something with that dog?" Alex asked with a baleful glance at Renfield, who was sitting placidly nearby.

"Is he bothering you?"

"Having him watch me with those crazy eyes makes me want to get a vaccination."

"That's how Renfield always looks at people, Uncle Alex," Holly said. "It means he likes you."

Taking Holly by the hand, Maggie left the house and speed-dialed a number on her cell phone on the way to her car. It was picked up immediately.

"Happy Thanksgiving," she heard her father say. Maggie grinned as she heard the familiar background sounds of barking dogs, crying babies, rattling dishes and pots, and an undertone of Perry Como crooning "Home for the Holidays."

"Hey, Dad. Happy Thanksgiving to you, too."

"You on the way to Bellingham now?"

"Well, actually no. I was wondering . . . do you think you could do without the mac and cheese this year?"

"That depends. Why am I having to do without it?"

"I was thinking about spending Thanksgiving here with some friends."

"Would one of them happen to be Mr. Ferry Ride?"

Maggie smiled ruefully. "Why do I always tell you too much?"

Her father chuckled. "You have a good day and call me later. And as for my mac and cheese, just put it in the freezer and bring it on your next visit."

"I can't, I have to serve it today. My friend . . . his name is Mark . . . incinerated the side dishes and blew up the turkey."

"So that's how he got you to stay? Smart man."

"I don't think it was on purpose," Maggie said, laughing. "Love you, Dad. Give Mom a kiss for me. And thanks for being so understanding."

"You sound happy, sweetheart," he said. "That makes me more thankful than anything."

I am happy, Maggie realized as she closed her

cell phone. She felt . . . buoyant. She guided Holly into the backseat of her car and leaned in to buckle the seat belt across the girl's chest and lap. As she adjusted the straps, her mind replayed the vision of the fire and smoke through the back-door window, and she couldn't help chuckling.

"Are you laughing because my uncles blew up the turkey?" Holly asked.

Maggie nodded, trying without success to stifle another chuckle.

Holly began to giggle. Her gaze met Maggie's, and she said innocently, "I didn't know turkeys could fly."

That cracked them both up, and they held on to each other, laughing, until Maggie had to dab at the corners of her eyes.

By the time Maggie and Holly returned to the house, Mark and Sam had cleaned up the disaster in the backyard and were in the kitchen peeling potatoes. Seeing Maggie, Mark came immediately to take the heavy parcel in her arms: a large foil pan weighted with enough sliced turkey to feed a dozen people. Holly followed with a large container of gravy. The scents of turkey roasted with sage, garlic, and basil wafted enticingly through the foil vents.

"Where did this come from?" Mark asked, setting the pan on one of the counters.

Maggie grinned at him. "It pays to have

connections. Elizabeth's son-in-law has a restaurant on Roche Harbor Road, and they're serving Thanksgiving dinner all day. So I called and ordered some turkey to go."

Bracing one hand on the counter, Mark looked down at her. Freshly showered and clean-shaven, he possessed a rough-and-ready handsomeness that stirred her senses.

The soft gruffness of his voice made her toes curl reflexively inside her boots. "Why aren't you on the ferry?"

"I changed my mind about going."

His mouth lowered to hers, offering a soft, searing pressure that brought hectic color to her face and took all the starch out of her knees. Blinking, Maggie realized that Mark had kissed her in front of his family. She frowned at him and glanced around his shoulder to see if they were watching, but Sam seemed absorbed in peeling potatoes, and Alex had taken it upon himself to start fluffing mixed greens in a large teak salad bowl. Holly was on the floor with Renfield, letting him lick the gravy lid.

"Holly," Maggie said, "make sure you throw that lid away after Renfield finishes. Do not put it back on the gravy."

"Okay. But my friend Christian says a dog's mouth is cleaner than a human's."

"Ask your uncle Mark," Sam said, "if he'd rather kiss Maggie or Renfield."

"Sam," Mark said in warning, but his younger brother grinned at him.

Snickering, Holly took the lid from Renfield and ceremoniously dropped it into the trash can.

Under Maggie's direction, the group managed to assemble a respectable Thanksgiving dinner, including the replacement dish of mac and cheese, sweet potato casserole, green beans, salad, turkey, and a simple dressing made with French bread crumbs, walnuts, and sage.

Sam opened a bottle of red wine and poured glasses for all the adults. Ceremoniously he gave Holly a wineglass filled with grape juice. "I'll make the first toast," he said. "To Maggie, for saving Thanksgiving." They all clinked glasses.

Maggie happened to glance at Holly, who was swirling and sniffing her grape juice in an exact imitation of Sam, who was sampling his wine. She saw that Mark had also noticed, and was biting back a grin. The sight had even brought a smile to Alex's brooding countenance.

"We can't just toast me," Maggie protested. "We need a toast for everyone."

Mark lifted his glass. "To the triumph of hope over experience," he said, and they all clinked again.

Maggie smiled at him. A perfect toast, she thought, on what had turned out to be a perfect day.

After dinner and a dessert of pie and coffee and milk for Holly, they cleared the dishes, cleaned the kitchen, and put the leftovers in covered containers. Sam turned on the television, found a football game, and stretched out on a recliner. Full and replete, Holly snuggled in a corner of the sofa and promptly fell asleep. Maggie covered her with a throw blanket and sat next to Mark at the other end of the sofa. Renfield went to his dog bed in the corner and flopped down with a grunt of contentment.

Although Maggie didn't care much about football one way or the other, she liked the ritual of watching a Thanksgiving game. It reminded her of all the Thanksgivings she had spent with her father and brothers, all of them hooting, moaning, and protesting the ref's calls.

Alex came to the doorway. "I'm heading out now," he said.

"Stay and watch the game," Sam said.

"We'll need help eating the leftovers," Mark added.

Alex shook his head. "Thanks, but I've had enough family time. Nice to meet you, Maggie."

"Nice to meet you, too."

Sam rolled his eyes after Alex had left. "Spreading joy and sunshine wherever he goes."

"With his marriage breaking up," Maggie said, "it's normal for him to go through a dark period."

The brothers seemed to find this highly amusing. "Honey," Mark said, "Alex has been in a dark period since the age of two."

Eventually Maggie found herself leaning in the crook of Mark's arm. His body was hard and warm, his shoulder supporting her head perfectly. She only half watched the game, the television screen a blur of color as she absorbed the feeling of being close to Mark.

"The mac and cheese," he said, "was even better than I had imagined."

"Secret ingredient."

"What is it?"

"I won't tell you mine unless you tell me yours."

There was a smile in his voice. "You first."

"I put a drizzle of truffle oil in the sauce. Now tell what you put in the coffee."

"A hint of maple sugar." He had taken her hand, his thumb stroking over the crests of her knuckles. The casual sensuality of his touch sent a deep, subtle quiver through her. She felt an equal measure of pleasure and despair, privately acknowledging that for a woman who had decided not to get involved, she had made a hell of a lot of questionable choices recently.

What was it Elizabeth had said? . . . That when it stopped feeling like flirting, that was when it became a problem. And it was impossible for Maggie to deny that it had gone beyond flirtation, far past the superficial. She could love him, if she let it happen. Deeply, passionately, ruinously.

He was the trap she had once desperately promised herself to avoid.

"I have to go," she whispered.

"No, stay." Mark looked into her eyes, and whatever he saw caused him to lift his hand to her cheek in the gentlest possible caress. "What is it?" he murmured.

Maggie shook her head and tried to force a smile, and pushed away from him. Every muscle tightened in protest as she left the warm comfort of his proximity. She went to Holly, who was still sleeping soundly, and bent to kiss her.

"Are you going?" Sam asked, levering himself out of the recliner.

"No need to get up," Maggie said, but Sam came to her and put his arms around her in a brotherly hug.

"You know," he said affably, "if you lose interest in my brother, I'm a refreshing alternative."

Maggie laughed and shook her head.

As Mark walked outside with Maggie, he was filled with desire and liking and sympathy, all bound with a thread of frustration. He understood the conflict within her, probably better than she would have believed. And he found himself in the position of having to push her, carefully, into something she was determined never to be ready for. If it were merely a question of being patient, he would have given her all the patience in the world. But that wouldn't be enough to get her past her fears.

He stopped her on the front porch, wanting to talk for a minute or two before they went out into the icy open breeze.

"Are you working at the shop tomorrow?" he asked.

Maggie nodded, not quite meeting his gaze. "It's going to be pretty busy from now until Christmas."

"How about dinner one night this week?"

That got her to look at him. Her eyes were soft and dark, her mouth edged with melancholy. "Mark, I . . ." She stopped and swallowed hard, and looked so woebegone that he instinctively reached for her. She stiffened, wedging her forearms between them, but he continued to hold her anyway. Their breaths mingled in puffs of steam.

"How come Sam got to hug you," Mark whispered, "and I don't?"

"Different kind of hug," she managed to say.

Mark lowered his forehead to hers. "Because you want me," he murmured.

Maggie didn't deny it.

A long moment passed, and she unfolded and slid her arms around him. "I'm not what you need," she said, her voice muffled in his sweater. "You need someone who can make a commitment to you and Holly. Someone who can be part of your family."

"You gave a pretty good impression of that today."

"I've been giving you mixed signals. I know that. I'm sorry." Maggie sighed, and her tone turned rueful. "Apparently you're too much temptation for me to withstand."

"You should just give in," he said kindly.

He felt a ripple of laughter run through her. But as she looked up at him, her breath caught on another laugh, he saw that her eyes were brilliant with unshed tears.

"God, please don't do that," he whispered. A single tear slipped down her cheek, and he wiped it with his thumb. "If you don't stop, Maggie, I'm going to make love to you right on this freezing porch with all the splinters."

Maggie buried her face against him, took a few deep breaths, and looked up at him again. "I probably seem like a coward," she said. "But I know my limitations. You don't know what I went through, watching my husband die slowly for more than a year. It nearly killed me. I can't do it again, ever. That was my one shot."

"Your one shot was over almost as soon as it started," Mark said, filled with impatient longing, loving the feel of her in his arms. "Your marriage never had a chance to get off the ground. You never had the mortgage, the dog, the kids, the arguments about whose turn it is to do the laundry." Glancing at the tremulous curve of her lower lip, he couldn't stop himself from kissing her, too hard and brief for pleasure. "Let's not do this right now. Come on, I'll walk you to the car."

They were both silent as he accompanied her to the Sebring. Maggie turned to face him, and he bracketed her face in his hands and kissed her again, this time letting his mouth linger until she made a soft sound in her throat and began to kiss him back.

Lifting his head, Mark smoothed her rambunctious curls and spoke in a voice roughened with affection. "Being alone isn't safety, Maggie. It's just being alone." And after she had climbed into the car, he closed the door carefully and watched her drive off.

Thirteen

· ·

To Maggie's relief, her relationship with Mark went back to normal the day after Thanksgiving. He brought coffee to the shop, and was so relaxed and charming that she could have almost believed that scene on his front porch had never happened.

On Monday, Maggie's day off, Mark asked her to help him shop for Christmas decorations since he and Sam had not even a single ornament to start with. Maggie accompanied him to various shops in Friday Harbor to advise on such items as fresh garlands for the mantels and doorways, a wreath for the front door, a set of heavy pillar candles on mercury glass stands, and a vintage framed Santa poster. The only thing Mark had balked at was a Williamsburg-style ornamental fruit pyramid as a centerpiece for the table.

"I hate fake fruit," Mark said.

"Why? It's beautiful. It's what the Victorians used for holiday decorating."

"I don't like anything that looks like I'm supposed to be able to eat it but can't. I'd rather have one made out of real fruit."

Maggie regarded him with amused exasperation. "It wouldn't last long enough. And if it's made out of real fruit and you eat it, what will you do then?"

"Buy more fruit."

After they had loaded the last of the purchases into his truck, Mark managed to talk Maggie into having dinner with him. She had tried to refuse, saying it was too much like going out, but he had wheedled, "It'll be just like lunch. Only later." And she had relented. They had gone to an intimate restaurant four miles out from Friday Harbor, sitting at a table near a fieldstone fireplace. In the glow of candlelight, they had eaten succulent Alaskan sea scallops stacked with duck confit and goat cheese, and filet mignon shimmering with a date espresso glaze.

"If this had been a date," Mark had told her afterward, "it would have been the best one of my life."

"It was good practice," Maggie had said with a laugh, "for when you really go out with someone."

But even to herself, she had sounded false and hollow.

During the weeks leading up to Christmas, the island bustled with holiday activities, concerts, celebrations, lighting contests, and festivals. What Holly looked forward to the most was the annual lighted boat parade. Held by the Friday Harbor Sailing Club and the San Juan Island Yacht Club, it was a flotilla of decorated and fully lit vessels that went from Shipyard Cove to the yacht club and back. Even the boaters who didn't join the parade strung their boats with lights. The last boat in the flotilla would be the Santa Ship, from which

Santa would disembark at the Spring Street dock. He would be met by musicians, and ride on a fire truck to the convalescent center.

"I want to watch it with you," Holly had told Maggie, who had promised she would walk to the dock after closing the shop, and meet them there.

The dock and surrounding area was massively crowded, however, and the cheerful clamor of parade-goers and carolers was near-deafening. Maggie wandered through the multitude, past clusters of families with children, and couples, and groups of friends. The lighted boats glittered and sparkled in the darkness, eliciting cries of excitement from the crowd. With a sinking heart, Maggie realized she wasn't going to be able to find Holly and Mark easily, if at all.

It was okay, she told herself. They would have a good time without her. She wasn't part of the family. If Holly was disappointed that she hadn't shown up, it wouldn't last for long.

But none of that helped to ease the tightness of Maggie's throat, or the pressure of anxiety in her chest. She kept searching through the crowd, past family after family.

She thought she heard her name in the tumult. Stopping, she turned and scanned her surroundings. She caught sight of a girl in a pink winter coat and a red hat. It was Holly, standing with Mark, waving to her. With a small gasp of relief, Maggie made her way to them.

"You missed some of the boats," Holly exclaimed, taking her hand.

"Sorry," Maggie said breathlessly. "It was hard to find you."

Mark smiled and put an arm around her shoulders, drawing her against his side. He glanced down at her face as he felt her drawing in deep draughts of air. "You okay?" he asked.

Maggie smiled and nodded, dangerously close to tears.

No, she thought. *I'm not okay.* She felt like she had just had one of those dreams in which she had been trying to find someone or something that was always out of reach, one of those stumbling-around, panicky nightmares. And now she was where she most wanted to be, with the two people in the world she most wanted to be with.

It felt so right that it scared her.

"You're sure you don't want to get a tree?" Mark asked the next Monday, as Maggie helped him to load a perfect Douglas fir onto his truck.

"I don't need one," she said cheerfully, sniffing the fresh traces of sap on her gloves while he tied the tree down. "I always spend Christmas in Bellingham."

"When are you leaving?"

"Christmas Eve." Seeing his slight frown, Maggie said, "Before I go, I'll leave a present for

Holly under the tree, so she can open it Christmas morning."

"She'd rather open it with you there."

Maggie blinked, uncertain how to reply. Did that mean he wanted her to spend Christmas with him? Was he thinking about inviting her? "I always stay with my family on Christmas," she said warily.

Mark nodded, letting the subject drop. He drove her to the house at Rainshadow Vineyard, and together they wrestled the tree inside.

It was quiet in the house, with Holly still at school. Sam had gone to Seattle to visit friends and to do some holiday shopping.

Maggie smiled as she saw the proliferation of white paper snowflakes hanging from doorways and ceilings. "Someone's been busy."

"Holly learned to make them in school," Mark said. "Now she's turned into a one-woman snowflake factory."

He started a fire in the fireplace, while Maggie unwrapped packages of white twinkle lights for the tree.

Within an hour, they had set the tree in its stand and strung it with lights. "Now for the magical part," Maggie said, wedging her way into the narrow space behind the tree. She plugged the light strand in, and the tree began to glimmer and sparkle.

"It's not magic," Mark said, but he was smiling as he stood back to view the tree.

"What is it, then?"

"A system of tiny bulbs illuminated by the movement of electrons in semiconductor material."

"Yes." Maggie held up a forefinger significantly as she approached him. "But what makes them *twinkle?*"

"Magic," he said in resignation, his lips twitching.

"Exactly." She gave him a satisfied grin.

Mark slid his hands through her hair and grasped her head, and looked at her. "I need you in my life."

For a moment Maggie couldn't move or breathe. The statement was startling in its bluntness, in its directness. She couldn't turn away, could only stare at him, mesmerized by the expression in his blue-green eyes.

"Not long ago I told Holly that love is a choice," Mark said. "I was wrong. Love isn't a choice. The only choice is what you're going to do with it."

"Please," she whispered.

"I understand what you're afraid of. I understand why this is so hard for you. And you can choose not to take a chance. But I'm going to love you anyway."

Maggie closed her eyes.

"You've got all the time you need," she heard him say. "I can wait until you're ready. I just had to tell you how I feel."

She still couldn't look at him. "I may never be ready for the kind of commitment you want. If you were just asking for meaningless sex, it would be no problem. That I could do. But you—"

"Okay."

Her eyes flew open. "Okay what?"

"I'll take the meaningless sex."

Maggie stared at him in bewilderment. "You just said you were willing to wait!"

"I'm willing to wait for commitment. But in the meantime I can settle for sex."

"So . . . you would be fine with a physical relationship that's going nowhere?"

"If that's your best offer."

Staring at him, Maggie saw the glint of laughter deep in his eyes. "You're jerking my chain," she said.

"No more than you're jerking mine."

"You don't think I'll go through with it, do you?"

"No," he said gently, "I don't."

Maggie was too worked up to be able to sort through the entire tangle of emotions inside her. There was indignation, fear, alarm, even a touch of amusement . . . but none of that was responsible for the vibrant, shivery heat that had begun to pump through her entire body. The sensation collected in places that deepened her flush and made her awareness of him unbearable. She wanted him, right then, with a stomach-lifting, heart-pounding, dizzying need.

Maggie was dimly amazed that her voice was steady as she asked, "Where's your bedroom?"

She had the satisfaction of seeing his eyes widen, the glint of amusement vanishing.

Mark led the way upstairs, glancing at her at intervals as if to make certain she was still with him. They went into his room, clean and sparely furnished, the walls painted a neutral color that was indistinguishable in the weak December daylight.

Before she could lose her nerve, Maggie stepped out of her shoes and stripped off her sweater and jeans. The cool air of the bedroom made her shiver as she stood there in her underwear. Mark approached her, and she lifted her head to see that he had taken off his sweater and T-shirt, his upper half bare and muscular and beautiful. His movements were careful, gentle, as if he was trying not to startle her. She could almost feel his gaze as it slid over her, coming to rest on her face.

"How beautiful you are," he whispered, letting one hand caress her shoulder. It seemed he took forever to finish undressing her, kissing every new inch of skin that was revealed.

Finally she lay naked on the bed, reaching up for him blindly. He dragged off his jeans and took her against him, his skin fever-hot beneath her exploring hands. He kissed her, his mouth artfully searching, then demanding, and she opened to him, yielding everything.

New sensations unfolded, pleasure surging in response to the clever explorations of his mouth, his gentle hands, the heat nearly overcoming her.

Bracing his weight over her, Mark smoothed her hair back from her perspiring face. "Did you really think it could be less than this?" he asked gently.

Maggie stared up at him, shaken to the depths of her soul. For them there could be nothing less than love, nothing less than forever. The truth was there in the mutual velocity of their pulses, the shocks of desire that resonated between them. She couldn't deny it any longer.

"Love me," she whispered, needing him, longing to possess him at last.

"Always. Maggie, love . . ." He entered her, a hot pressure that filled her in an inexorable slide. He was so strong, inside her, over her. She felt the waves of pleasure rising higher, tipping back slightly, then forward again, higher, until she cried out in wonder. Her hands groped over his back, the sweat-slicked muscles bunching hard beneath her palms. He followed her, finding his own release in the sweet, strong harbor of her embrace.

Afterward they lay together in transcendent silence, their bodies pressed intimately close.

There were more questions that would be asked, answers that would have to be found. But for now all that could wait, while she lay steeped in a sense of newness and possibility. And hope.

Fourteen

CHRISTMAS EVE

Some of the wrapped presents had to be moved while Alex and Sam set up the electric train to circle around the Christmas tree. Holly crowed in delight, running around in her red flannel pajamas to follow the train's progress. Renfield crept forward and watched suspiciously.

It had been agreed that Holly could open one present on Christmas Eve, and the rest would wait until the morning. Naturally she had chosen the largest box, which had turned out to be the train set. Another box, still neatly wrapped, contained a fairy house that Maggie had started for her, along with paint, bags of dried moss and flowers, a jar of glitter glue, and other materials for Holly to decorate it with.

Mark sat on the sofa next to Maggie, who was straightening a pile of Christmas books they had read aloud.

"It's getting late," Maggie murmured. "I should be going soon." Her nerves prickled pleasantly as he leaned over to speak quietly into her ear.

"Spend the night here with me."

Maggie smiled. "I thought there was a no-sleepover rule," she whispered.

"Yes, but there's an exception: A guest can sleep over if you're going to marry her."

She gave him an admonishing glance. "You're being pushy again, Nolan."

"Do you think so? Then you're probably not going to like one of the presents I'm giving you tomorrow morning."

Her heart skipped a beat. "Oh, God." She put her head in her hands. "Don't let it be what I think it is." She looked at him through her fingers.

Mark smiled at her. "I have reason to hope. You've had a hard time saying no to me lately."

Which was more or less true. Maggie lowered her hands and stared at him, this handsome, impossibly sexy man who had changed her entire life in such a short time. She felt a rush of happiness, so strong that she could hardly breathe. "That's only because I love you," she said.

He reached for her, his head bending over hers, his mouth firm and sweet.

"Euw," she heard Holly exclaim, giggling. "They're kissing again!"

"We have only one choice," Sam told her. "We'll go upstairs so we don't have to see them."

"Is it my bedtime?"

"It's a half hour past your bedtime."

Holly's eyes widened. "Santa's coming soon. We have to set out the cookies and milk."

"And don't forget the carrots for the reindeer,"

Maggie said, disentangling herself from Mark and heading into the kitchen with Holly.

"Do you think Renfield might scare Santa?" Holly asked, her voice drifting back to the living room.

"With all the dogs Santa's seen? No way . . ."

Standing and stretching, Alex said, "I'm outta here. It's my bedtime, too."

"You're coming back tomorrow morning, right?" Sam asked.

"Is Maggie cooking breakfast?"

"At least in a supervisory capacity."

"I'll be here, then." Alex went to the doorway and paused to look back at them. "I like this," he surprised them by saying reflectively. "It feels sort of . . . family-ish."

He went to say good-bye to Holly and Maggie, and left.

"I think he'll be okay," Sam remarked. "Especially when the divorce is final."

Mark smiled slightly. "I think we'll all be okay."

Holly came back into the room and set a plate of cookies and a glass of milk on the coffee table. "Renfield," she said, "do *not* eat any of that."

The bulldog wagged his back end agreeably.

"Come on, gingersnap," Sam said. "I'll tuck you in upstairs."

Holly looked at Mark and Maggie. "Will you come kiss me good night?"

"In just a few minutes," Maggie promised.

"We're just going to pick up a little and get things ready for tomorrow." She watched fondly as Holly scampered up the stairs.

As Mark went to turn the train off, Maggie went to the plate of cookies and took out from her pocket a slip of paper.

"What's that?" he asked, coming back to her.

"A note that Holly wanted to put next to the plate." She showed it to him. "Do you know what she meant by this?"

Dear Santa

thank you for making my wish come true.

love
Holly

Mark set the note on the coffee table, and put his arms around her. "Yes," he said, looking into her soft brown eyes. "I know what she meant."

And as he bent his head and kissed her, Mark Nolan finally believed in magic.

Center Point Publishing
600 Brooks Road ● PO Box 1
Thorndike ME 04986-0001 USA

(207) 568-3717

US & Canada:
1 800 929-9108
www.centerpointlargeprint.com